CW01431280

The World at His Feet

A DI Alex Jamieson Mystery

Peter Darling

Useful Publishing
Independent Thinking

www.usefulpublishing.com.au

The World at His Feet – A DI Alex Jamieson Mystery

Copyright © 2023 by Useful Publishing

First edition November 2023

All rights reserved.

No part of this publication may be reproduced, distributed or transmitted in any form or by any means, including photocopying, recording or other electronic or mechanical methods, without the prior written permission of the publisher, except as permitted by U.S. copyright law. For permission requests, please contact email: hello@usefulpublishing.com.au or go to the website.

The story, all names, characters and incidents portrayed in this production are fictitious. No identification with actual persons (living or deceased), places, buildings and products is intended or should be inferred.

Book Cover by 100Covers

Book Text Typography by Useful Publishing

About the Author

Peter Darling

Peter lives in Aylesbury, England, which sits about 30 miles to the north west of London.

He is married to Caroline and they have two kids, Thomas and Lily.

Peter thrives on popular culture – music, tv, books, sport and cinema and for his sins has been an ardent follower of Chelsea FC for over 50 years through the thin and thick and now, in 2023, thin again!

'Having one novel published was an absolute dream but now a second one goes beyond that. I'm having the time of my life creating people and conducting their lives. It must be the God complex in me coming out! Thanks again to my publishers - I owe you a beer!'

So, here's to my big brother, Mike, and his wife Claire. As soppy as it sounds he's probably the best brother you could ever wish for – keep smiling.

And to John for everything he's done for Caroline and I and the kids – its always appreciated by each and every one of us – thank you so much.

And finally to anyone who is struggling – keep going God Bless!

Contents

Prologue

Wednesday 11th November - 19:40

Emergency services. Which service do you require?
Ambulance. It's my son. He's been st.......
Putting you through.
Ambulance Control Room. My name is Mary. I am your call handler. Can I take the number that you are calling from, please?
07844 712714
What is your exact location, please?
Um, I'm on the corner of Rankin Avenue, where it meets Holmes Road.
Ok. Do you have the what3words app on your phone?
Yes.
Can you activate it and tell me the three words, please?
For fuck's sake, ok, hold on, hold on. Ok, so curtain - Sunday - dial - please hurry.
Curtain - Sunday - dial. I've sent those details to the attending crew. They will be with you as soon as they possibly can. What has happened?
Move. MOVE.

They will be with you as soon as possible. I need you to stay calm. Can you tell me what has happened?

My son has been stabbed.

Ok. Is anyone else involved? Is there anyone else there?

No. I've just found him lying on the pavement.

How old is your son?

He's 16.

And would you say that he is normally quite fit?

Yes. He is always playing football. He's very fit.

Ok. The ambulance is nearly with you. You are doing brilliantly. What is your son's name?

Ashley.

And yours?

Holly. Holly Matthews.

Ok, Holly, how is Ashley's breathing? Is he conscious?

He's, he's moaning. His eyes are opening and closing.

You said he was stabbed. Can you tell where the injury is?

It's his left thigh.

Is there any severe bleeding?

Yes, oh God, yes. There's blood pumping out of his fucking leg. It's all over the place.

Ok. The ambulance is very close. Are you wearing a belt?

A belt? Yes. Why?

I want you to take it off and use it as a tourniquet if you can. You are doing brilliantly.

Ok, the belt is off. What now?

I want you to try and get it between the wound on Ashley's leg and his chest and get it as tight as possible. Does that make sense?

Ok, ok.

Have you managed to do that?

I think so. He's still bleed..........I can see blue lights behind me.

Ok. Just make sure that the belt is as tight as you can make it. The crew will be there in a minute.

Ok.

Hello love, we'll take it from here. Just go with my colleague there. We'll look after him now.

Holly. You've done so well. I'll leave you with the crew now. I hope Ashley will be ok.

Chapter One

Wednesday 11th November – 21:10

Alex Jamieson stood back from the general hubbub and watched as events unfurled.

He checked his watch—ten past nine. Half an hour ago, he was sitting in front of the television watching a Champions League match. Then came the call from Claire Evason, duty DS for tonight.

'Sir, we've got a case. It's a bad one. I'm on my way, and I'll be with you in ten minutes. Then another ten, fifteen minutes to the scene.'

Jamieson hauled himself up from the sofa, went upstairs to put on the suit that he'd only an hour or so ago taken off and waited for the sound of Evason's car arriving.

He texted Lucy, Mrs Jamieson, who was at the gym and told her not to wait up and that he'd see her later.

Such was the life of an on-duty DI. But he'd signed up for this and, in a perverse way, what he lived for.

Evason gave the briefest of toots on the car horn, and Jamieson was out and in the passenger seat within seconds.

'What have we got, Claire?' he asked.

'A stabbing, Sir. Sixteen-year-old boy.'

Jamieson's heart lurched. Another stabbing. Another young life stubbed out. Countrywide knife crime was at an all-time high. And no matter what the powers that be did, there seemed to be no way of halting the crisis. Jamieson's son, Justin, was sixteen, and it was all Jamieson could do not to think 'there but by the grace of God'.

'Who called it in?'

'The Mother, Sir'

'So, she was with him when it happened?'

'No, Sir. She found him lying on the pavement and called the emergency services.'

'Close to home then?' asked Jamieson.

'Not particularly, perhaps a couple of miles.'

'How did Mum just happen upon her son then?'

'Unclear at present. Here we are.' Evason flashed her warrant card at the officer manning the cordoned-off area. The officer directed her to a space where she could park.

They were out within seconds and striding towards the white-suited SOCO teams. A gentle rain had started, although it remained unseasonably warm.

'Claire', said Jamieson ', You do what you need to do. I'm going to stand back and watch how things develop.'

Evason nodded. She had worked with Jamieson long enough to know that he was not one to jump in with both size 12s. He was a thinker. He would take a more cerebral approach.

Jamieson watched as Evason sought out the scene of crimes manager Lisa Wooster. Jamieson was pleased. He had worked with Wooster on many occasions. He knew she was excellent at her job, committed, hardworking, and a good communicator. Still, woe betides anyone who infringed upon her crime scene without the appropriate white crime suit and shoe coverings, including Detective Inspectors.

Jamieson took in the scene.

The incident occurred at the junction of two roads, just everyday residential streets that could be almost anywhere in the country. The cordoned-off area covered both roads. Behind the police tape, the usual onlookers had gathered. Jamieson could never determine whether these individuals were ghouls who were there in the absence of anything decent on the television or were genuinely interested in what had happened and, more importantly, what they could do to prevent it from happening in the future.

In truth, there wasn't much to see. The victim had long gone, and even the increasingly heavy rain was fast washing away the blood that had been shed.

There were a dozen or so crime scene officers all doing something. Jamieson didn't know what exactly, but he did know that these officers were integral in the early stages of the investigation. In these early hours, discoveries were often made, which pushed the case in favour of the prosecution.

There were three police cars and a minibus that had bought in the majority of the SOCO team. Now and again, a police car would trigger a lazy blue light that would fleetingly illuminate the scene.

Jamieson watched Evason as she confidently moved among her peers, referring to Wooster, interested in what everyone was doing and why adding her own value wherever she felt it would help. Then, finally, she took a call, raised her head and located him, making her way over.

'So, the call to the emergency services was made around twenty to eight, and the crew were here within four minutes. The Team Leader was an experienced paramedic, and he could see what the likely outcome was going to be. He called a backup crew to take the Mother to the hospital as he didn't want her to witness her sixteen-year-old son either bleed out or arrest in the back of an ambulance. In the event, they got the lad into A&E, but he arrested almost straight away. They tried CPR, but the senior physician called it at around eight-thirty. We got the call not long after.'

Jamieson pushed his hand through his hair: 'Where's Mum now?'

'Heavily sedated. They've kept her in.' Evason said, and before Jamieson could ask, 'The senior physician has categorically said that there is no way we are speaking to her tonight.'

Jamieson knew that was the right course of action but was still frustrated.

'So when can we speak to her?'

'Probably after nine in the morning. Subject to confirmation from a senior doctor. Lisa Wooster has sent one of her team to the hospital to bag up clothing and collect other possible evidence. The hospital has, at least, agreed to that.'

'And here?' said Jamieson, gesturing towards the crime scene.

'They'll be here a while yet. No sign of any weapon yet, though.'

Jamieson puffed out his cheeks: 'Ok, let's get the team in for seven thirty tomorrow. It looks like you and I will be at the hospital. With any luck, Tilly Jenner will be the pathologist responsible for the autopsy. So we can kill two birds with one stone,' He winced at the word 'kill' 'then Sandy and Rog can start putting some background to our victim.'

Evason unlocked the car and went to find Wooster to arrange a catch-up for the following day. Jamieson eased himself into the passenger seat with a feeling of foreboding.

'Kids,' he thought to himself, 'I hate it when it's kids.'

Chapter Two

Thursday 18th November – 07:45

The rain from the previous evening had continued into the following morning, only it had become much harder, and the temperature had dropped considerably.

This meant that Jamieson's journey into work would take longer than he had anticipated. Wet weather meant reduced road speeds which meant more waits at traffic lights - all of which lessened potential accidents - but didn't get a Detective Inspector to a meeting he'd arranged on time.

By the time he had parked up and reached the team's office on the second floor, it was nearly a quarter to eight - fifteen minutes late - not a good start.

The room had been set out in the obligatory murder format or any other significant enquiry. That is, a horseshoe of chairs facing a whiteboard, where details of the investigation would be entered. So far, the name and age of the deceased had been written and circled in the centre of the board. On a branch from the circle leading off to the left were details of how, when and where the incident occurred. On another branch directly above the deceased's details was the name Holly Matthews and the date of birth 15/1/1982.

So far, that was it, but the board would fill with more information as the enquiry progressed - at least, that was the theory.

'Sorry, sorry.' said Jamieson as he entered the room, his hands raised in mock surrender.

He swooped onto a takeout cup of coffee that someone, probably Roger Johnson, had left on his desk and took a much-needed mouthful. A couple of times a day, the team allowed themselves the luxury of coffee from Giorgio's, the nearest and best local coffee provider. The remainder of the time, it was what passed for coffee, from the station machine down the corridor, or nothing - nothing was the preferred option unless desperation had taken hold.

'Claire', said Jamieson, 'why don't we begin.'

Claire Evason moved front and centre with her usual grace and minimal effort. She was in her early thirties and had been a Detective Sergeant for nearly four years. She had entered the police on a graduate scheme and had impressed to date. Jamieson knew she had designs on a DI role at some future point. He also knew that the expectation was that to reach DI, a candidate should have a rounded experience of working in different areas; the Met was always a firm favourite. It looked good on a CV and that sooner rather than later, he would lose her from his team - a fantastic opportunity for her (which he instinctively believed she would and should take) but not so good for Bedfordshire Constabulary. Losing people of Evason's calibre would be a wrench.

'Not a great deal to go on yet', began Evason. 'Ashley James,16, died of a stab wound to the upper thigh at eight thirty yesterday evening. His Mother had made the 999 call at around twenty to eight. Ashley died in hospital.'

'As you can see,' Evason indicated the board behind her. 'Mother is Holly Matthews. She followed in a second ambulance. She collapsed when she was told that Ashley had died and has remained in the hospital under heavy sedation. We should be able to speak to her this morning with the doctors' permission.'

'Ashley was found lying on the pavement by his Mother with no one else around. Initial local enquiries have not discovered anything or anyone of interest. The area is not affluent. There are very few who live there who can afford CCTV, although some will have doorbell cameras which might help. Door to door is in the area for the foreseeable future to see what might be thrown to light.'

'Finally,' continued Evason ', there is no trace of a likely murder weapon. Ashley had two mobile phones on him - an iPhone and a basic model phone. Initial thoughts from tech are that the iPhone was for personal use and the other was some type of burner - any calls and messages have been deleted on the burner.'

'Is that a known district for drug use?' This from Roger Johnson, the newest member of the team. He had been seconded for a previous case and had done well. Jamieson asked and, to his surprise, was permitted for Johnson to join the team full-time, subject to a six-month probation. Johnson had jumped at the chance and was studying for his Sergeant's exams. He had been a good addition.

Jamieson fielded the question: 'Like all of these estates, there is a degree of drug users in that area. What's your thinking, Rog?'

'Well, the burner phone gives it a gang or county lines kind of feel.' Jamieson liked that the young man was fearless in airing his views in front of his seniors. Some he knew of would hold back in a situation like this to avoid the risk of sounding stupid.

'It's an avenue to pursue without a doubt. Sandy, any ideas?'

Pete Stone, Sandy, to everyone, was the final member of the team. 'We'll need to gather a hell of a lot of information on both the lad and his Mum before we make too many assumptions, Alex'. Stone was the elder statesman of the team. He was the only one who called Jamieson by his given name, this was not an issue to Jamieson, but he did wonder whether Stone did it to remind the others that he was their senior, not necessarily by rank, but certainly in experience.

Stone was in his early fifties and was a seasoned, well-regarded Detective Sergeant. The last major case the team handled tested Stone's resilience to the core. He had come through, but the cost had been heavy to the relationship with his wife of over a quarter of a century. Margaret had moved out of the marital home and in with a male friend. No one was entirely sure whether that was it for the marriage or whether some breathing space was required. Recently though, rumour had it that Stone and Margaret were trying to patch things up and that a possible reconciliation was in the air. Nobody was brave enough to ask Stone direct.

'Absolutely', said Jamieson. 'Anything more, Claire?'

'No sign of Holly's mobile even though she used it to call emergency services and appears not to have moved until she was put in the ambulance. It still may come to light, I guess,' replied Evason. 'Oh, and Holly has a police record going back a few years. Drugs, D&D, shoplifting, and other more minor public offences. Ashley is clean.'

'Ok,' said Jamieson ', so a plan of action. Claire and I will interview Holly at the hospital and hopefully take care of the meeting with the pathologist.' He looked at Evason. 'Is it Tilly?' She nodded. 'Good.'

Jamieson had worked with Tilly Jenner in the past and found her to be accommodating and not frightened to express an early view in the cases that she dealt with. Some of her male counterparts would not say an early cause of death even if there were a bullet hole and a smoking gun in the vicinity.

'Sandy, you and Rog, get down to the school and see if you can get a picture of Ashley. What was he like? Who were his close mates? You know the score. Also, see if you can get more background on Holly. I wonder whether Social Services have ever been involved? Let's try to understand the dynamics of all of this, which might push us in the right direction.'

People started to gather up their things, ready to brave the elements outside.

Jamieson looked at his watch: 'Let's meet back here for, shall we say, four o'clock?'

They shuffled out, ready to make some sense of it all.

Chapter Three

Thursday 12th November – 08:55

'Oh Christ', thought Helen Miller. 'What a bloody mess!'

She stood looking out the office window as the rain continued to teem down.

Kids hurried in with their coats on and their hoods up. There was no time to spend in the playground because of the weather, which was a problem. If the kids had been able to gather in the playground, then news of what had happened would be out there and spread like wildfire, but then at least everyone would know. Now they would find out piecemeal. She would have to get them all into the hall for an impromptu assembly so that a consistent message would be delivered. It was, to say the least, a horrible day.

Helen was only acting Headteacher. Edwin Morris-Jones was the actual Headteacher, but he was on a sabbatical.

'Sabbatical', she said the word out loud in a faux hippy voice. 'Suh-bar-tical'

God, Morris-Jones was forty-two and had only been doing the job for three years, and he needed a suh-bar-tical already. He was probably on a kibbutz somewhere, re-finding or redefining himself when he should be here dealing with this situation.

There was a knock on the door. Judith, the school sec-retary, poked her head round: 'There are two policemen here. If possible, they would like to have ten minutes of your time.'

Helen checked her watch.

'I can give them ten minutes at the very most. Can you let the Heads of Year know there will be an assembly at ten past nine, please? We need to get the message across as soon as we can.'

She massaged her temples. Ever since her mobile had rung at eleven fifteen yesterday evening, there had been a steady buildup of pressure. She had immediately mo-bilised her senior management team. She advised them of the tragic events and how things would need to be handled this morning.

There was another knock on the door.

'Come', said Helen, suddenly realising that she was in teacher mode. 'Sorry, I mean, come in.'

Stone and Johnson appeared. They had been caught in an even heavier downpour between the car and the entrance to the school and were looking somewhat bedraggled.

'Good morning', said Stone. 'I'm DS Stone, and this is DS Johnson. We'd appreciate some of your time to talk about Ashley James.' Johnson was pleased and a little surprised to hear that Stone had dropped the by-now obligatory 'acting' before his introduction.

'Yes. Of course,' said Helen. 'Please take off your wet coats and have a seat. I'm sure Judith has mentioned that I only have until ten past nine, then I have to go and deliver an assembly. But, to be truthful, I'm really not sure what I am going to say.'

As she spoke, she indicated two school-sized chairs facing the Headteacher's wide desk.

Johnson took Stone's coat and hung both on a stand in the corner. He then joined Stone in the remaining empty chair opposite Helen Miller; it reminded him of his frequent visits to the Headmaster during his own primary school years.

'Firstly, we are so sorry that this has happened. It can't be an easy day for anyone.' Stone began, 'We're trying to build up a picture of what sort of lad Ashley was. It will help us moving forward from where we are.'

Helen considered her reply: 'Ashley was….um…look...if you could create an individual, a young person if you like, who epitomised how you wanted your school to be viewed by the outside world, then that was Ashley. If we were the type of school to have a Head Boy, we're not, by the way, but without a doubt, it would have been him. He was kind, considerate, funny, loyal.....' she paused. Suddenly a wave of emotion hit her, and she let out a sob. Tears came, and she scrambled for a box of tissues on the desk in front of her. She mopped at her eyes and tried to regain some composure.

Stone was up and round the other side of the desk. He had crouched to her level and gently patted her shoulder. He looked her in the eye as he consoled her.

Having recovered her composure, Helen said, 'I am so sorry about that. How unprofessional of me.' Her voice was still thick with emotion, and her nose was snotty and red.

'Not at all,' said Stone. 'You've had a shock. Everyone involved has. It comes out when you least expect it.'

'It's just that I saw Ash yesterday; he was his usual funny self. Yet, less than twenty-four hours later, I'm referring to him in the past tense....he was sixteen. How on earth can that be right?' Helen looked to Stone for an answer.

He simply said, 'It isn't. Now, if you're up to it, I'm going to fire a few quick questions at you, and then we'll go and deliver your assembly with you.'

Helen looked at him: 'You'd do that?'

Stone nodded.

In all honesty, the last thing he wanted to do was stand up in front of three hundred and sixty grieving teenagers, but there was no way the woman in front of him could do it. She would probably need as much counselling as some of them would. She had a vested personal interest in this situation. He didn't.

'Ok, so Ashley', said Stone. 'Academically?'

'Just completed GCSEs - nine straight A*s.'

'A-levels? University?'

She looked at him. Clearly, Stone hadn't been told: 'Well, he had started an A-level course with us, and he would have been a candidate for any of the top universities....' she paused. '.....but we didn't expect him to be with us after Christmas.'

Stone looked puzzled: 'Why's that?'

'He would have been seventeen just before Christmas. He was going to sign with one of the big football clubs. He was going to be a professional footballer.'

'Ah', Stone and Helen looked at Johnson. He had the palm of his hand against his forehead. 'I read about him in the local paper. I didn't associate with the name. Dozens of clubs wanted to sign him, including a couple of the big Spanish boys, but his Dad had always maintained that nothing would happen until he was seventeen.'

Helen nodded.

'Plays down at Akley FC, I think?' said Johnson. 'A seriously good prospect. The Nationals were talking about him being one of the best. Future International.'

Stone checked his watch: 'Two more questions. Parents?'

Helen shrugged: 'Dad lives in Spain. Something to do with football. He comes back regularly to see Ash. Mum? I don't know much about her. She never comes to the school. Dad always comes back for parents' evening. I have heard rumours, but I'm not going to pass them on. I'm sure you'll find out what you need about her.'

Stone nodded: 'Fair enough. 'He paused: 'It is important that I ask this last question. Please don't take offence; we need to get a full picture to work out exactly what has happened.'

Stone looked Helen in the eye to check that she understood. She looked uncertain but nodded.

'Are there any circumstances in which Ashley would have been involved in gangs or drugs?'

Helen considered her answer: 'I'd say not......but I would add that Ash was fiercely loyal. I think he had a younger brother and two younger sisters - four and six. They came first, and I believe he would have done anything to ensure the family remained together. But, again, I would stress that this is my opinion from what I have seen and know of him; however, there is no evidence to say that he was involved in either gangs or drugs.'

'Thanks', said Stone. 'We may need to come back, but it will be easier then, less raw.'

They stood to leave. Johnson was first up and out of the door. As Stone followed, Helen gently pulled him back.

She stood in front of him and took both of his hands in hers.

She looked him in the eye: 'Thank you,' she said, 'For what you've done and what you're about to do. It means a tremendous amount.'

Then she did a strange thing; she kissed him on the cheek and gave a resigned smile and a slight shrug: 'I guess that's the second unprofessional thing I've done in the last ten minutes!'

Stone followed her out of the room. He felt a little speechless, which was not a good thing when he was just about to address three hundred and sixty pupils with probably one of the worse bits of news they had ever heard.

Chapter Four

Thursday 12th November – 09:50

The hospital had confirmed that Holly Matthews was fit enough for an interview, but for how long, they couldn't say.

'She's in shock', said the doctor. 'I'm not even sure that the events of last night have sunk in fully.'

'I need to talk to her.' Insisted Jamieson, 'I have a fit young man lying dead in the pathology lab, and I need to begin to piece together exactly what happened. Ms Matthews is key to us finding out.'

'I understand, Detective Inspector, and I'm just pointing out that the fit young man *was* her son. She is still processing the fact that she will never see him alive again, so you will need to bear that in mind and tread carefully please.'

Holly was on a side ward. A uniformed officer had been placed just outside the door. Nobody thought anything would happen, but it was standard protocol in these situations.

Jamieson and Evason approached, and the officer stood. Evason told her to relax and asked if there was anything of note to report. The answer was no, although the mobile phone hadn't turned up yet. Holly had been sedated for most of the night and came around just before six. She was aware of what had happened and had sat sobbing for the last four hours. Her Mother was at home looking after the little girls, and the boy, Lewis, had been with his Father for the last few days.

The doctor had already confirmed that there was nothing physically wrong with Holly and that she would be discharged from their care later today. Her Mother would be coming up on the bus later - there was no money in the kitty for a taxi and no spare hospital transport for physically able patients - so it would be a return journey on the bus as well.

Jamieson took Evason aside: 'She can't go home on a damn bus. Look at the state of her.'

They both peered around the door. A woman of indeterminate age - she could have been fifteen, she could have been seventy-five - sat in a chair beside a hospital bed. Her face was puffy from crying. She hugged herself and rocked gently back and forth.

'Find out what time her Mum will be here and get the officer outside to arrange an unmarked car to take them home. Anyone kicks up a fuss about people using the police as a bloody taxi service, tell them to bill me or better still, come and look the lass in there in the eye and tell her that her son's life isn't worth the cost of a ten-minute journey in a police car.'

Jamieson stepped into the room 'Holly', he said, his voice little more than a whisper.

Holly lifted her head, a look of expectation and hope on her face. Surely this man was here to tell her that it had all been a mistake and that Ashley was waiting at home for her. Please!

He spoke again: 'Holly, my name is Detective Inspector Jamieson. I am so sorry about Ashley. I want to find out what happened for both him and you. I will need to talk to you for a while. Do you think that would be alright?'

Evasion came in: 'This is my colleague, Claire; she will be helping me. Is it ok if she stays?'

Holly nodded slowly and returned to her rocking.

Jamieson looked around and found a chair which he pulled up close to Holly. Evason stood further away. 'So, Holly,' he said, 'what happened yesterday evening?'

The girl sniffed and looked straight ahead of her. She spoke quietly and forced herself to remember what she had seen. Occasionally she would punctuate with a sniff or a sob: 'I dunno. I was following Ash, and then I found him on the pavement. He was bleeding...there was so much blood. I dunno what had happened. I phoned 999, and they sent an ambulance. I did something with my belt, the woman told me, but I can't really remember what. They put Ash in the ambulance and told me I couldn't go with him. Then there was another ambulance, and I went in that. When I got to the hospital, people were running around everywhere, but I saw them in slow motion...that doesn't make any sense, I know, but it's what I remember. They put me in a room with a policewoman and gave me a cup of tea. Then a man came in wearing green and told me that he was sorry, but there was nothing they could do and that Ash was dead. I said that can't be right; he was only sixteen, you don't die when you're only sixteen. The man said sorry again and that he would give me something to help and arrange for me to stay in hospital for the night. The next thing I knew, I woke up in the hospital bed. I'm sorry I can't really focus. I think my Mum is supposed to be coming. Do you know where she is?'

She was beginning to get over-animated.

'Your Mum is on her way. She'll be here soon,' said Jamieson and made eyes at Evason as if to say, 'find out when they think she'll be here.'

'I can't believe any of it.' Said, Holly. 'I keep thinking that someone's gonna come in and say it's ok and that there's been a mistake and that Ash has been at football training all this time.'

'Holly,' began Jamieson ', you mentioned that you were following Ash. Can you remember why that was?'

The girl paused as if she ought not to answer that but then decided that she should: 'He'd had a lot of money recently, and I mean a lot, he would buy presents for his brother and sisters, new trainers at a hundred quid a pop, that sort of thing. I didn't know where he got it, and he wouldn't tell me. He'd tell me to chill and that it was ok because he'd be signing for one of the big boys soon, and money would be no problem.'

'So, you followed him?'

'I'd got this App on his mobile from when he was a little boy. That was a condition of him having a mobile phone when he was thirteen. He'd forgotten I'd got it installed. It tracked him in real-time. So I knew exactly where he was. That's how I found him so quick.'

'And you saw nobody else whilst you were out?' Asked Jamieson.

'No, I don't think so. It had started raining, and wasn't a very nice evening.' Holly shook her head as she spoke as if to reaffirm her answer.

Jamieson rubbed his chin: 'One last question for now, if that's ok, Holly? You said that Ash said he'd be 'signing for one of the big boys'. What did he mean by that?'

'That's his football', she said. 'He would have been seventeen in December. That was when his Dad said he could sign professionally. I don't know much about football, but I'd heard of all the clubs who had said there were interested. His Dad takes care of that side of things. Jayce is a pretty laid-back guy, but even he was excited by it all. He'd say, 'the sky's the limit for the boy, Hol.' Then with sudden urgency, 'Does Jayce know yet?'

Suddenly the door burst open, and a big woman in her sixties bundled through, followed by a harassed-looking Evason. Evason spread her hands in a helpless gesture: 'Sorry, she wouldn't wait.'

Jamieson shrugged back as if to say, 'no problem.'

'Holly Baby, Holly Baby' shouted the woman running toward the startled girl and smothering her in her ample bosom. She then rounded on Jamieson: 'Who the fuck do you think you are harassing my daughter at a time like this. You should be ashamed of yourself. Can't you see that she's not fit to speak to anyone, let alone hounded by the police?'

Holly pushed her Mother away. "Mum, Mum, it's not like that. They're trying to help, is all. They're trying to find out what happened. Does Jayce know? Have you told him? He should know.'

'I've not told him,' said the big woman. 'Why would I have his number? It's not like you've been with him for fifteen years since he walked out on you.'

Christ thought Jamieson, their son and grandson, was lying dead in the mortuary, and they're bickering about whether the boy's Father should be told. In truth, he'd got all he needed out of Holly for the time being, and now the Mother was here, the dynamic had changed. Holly was right, though; Jason James needed to be told and quickly. It wouldn't be fair on the man to hear something like this second or even third-hand.

"Holly,' said Jamieson 'we're going to leave now, but we will need to talk again soon. Claire here is going to give you details of family liaison, and they will be in touch later today to let you know what they can do to help.....'

'We don't need your help,' snarled Mrs Mathews, senior.

'For fuck's sake Mum, shut up.' Holly turned to Jamieson 'Will you tell Jason what has happened, please? He should know. His number is on my mobile...shit.' It suddenly dawned on her that her mobile was missing. 'Oh no, no .....try Dave at Akley Football Club. He'll have his number, but please do it soon. He should know.'

Evason skirted around Mrs Matthews Senior and handed Holly two business cards: 'One for family liaison, but they will be round yours later today anyway. The other is mine. Please call anytime if you need to. Can you also get yourself another mobile.....'

"You can get hold of her on mine' interjected Mrs Matthews Senior.

Evason ignored the interruption '......and let me have the number as soon as you have it. We'll try our best to speak to Jason before he hears from anyone else.'

She went to leave and then turned back: 'Oh, if your original mobile phone turns up, please let us know.' She looked Holly directly in the eye. 'We are really so sorry about Ashley.'

Jamieson said: 'I've arranged for a police car to take you home when you're ready.' And he followed Evason out of the door.

Behind him, he heard the not-so-subtle voice of Mrs Matthews Senior: 'I dunno, these people using the police like they're a bloody taxi service!'

On the way out, Jamieson debated whether to take a five-minute detour and get the outline results of the post-mortem. It would mean they would be delayed in their attempt to contact Jason James, but he decided it was worth the slight wait.

They found the pathology lab and Dr Jenner's office. She was sitting behind a computer typing into a template document.

Jamieson stuck his head round the door: 'Tilly', he said.

'Oh, Alex. Not quite finished yet.' Although theirs was a working relationship, they used an informal means of addressing each other. Jamieson found it made the subject matter slightly less daunting.

'We're in a real rush. Just looking for a heads-up, really. You know, edited highlights.'

'Ok', said Tilly referring to the computer screen: 'So we're looking at a mixed-race male sixteen years of age. This was an incredibly fit individual, fantastic muscle definition, minimal fat content, all internal organs healthy.....' She looked at Alex. 'An elite athlete of some sort?'

Alex nodded: 'A footballer.'

Tilly continued: '.....cause of death was a loss of blood leading to a cardiac arrest. Blood loss as a result of a wound to the left femoral artery. The weapon that made the wound was not one of these gang-type zombie knives; the entry wound would have been much bigger and caused a tear in the muscle; no, this was a much more regular knife, perhaps something you'd find in the kitchen.'

'The femoral artery is a major supply of blood around the body. It is protected by fat, muscle and the femur, the thigh bone. It's incredibly bad luck to miss all that and get to the artery. It really is.'

'Ok, thanks', said Alex 'anything more to add?'

Tilly sighed: 'Only that it is very sad. Cut down before the prime of his life.'

'Yep', said Alex, and after a thoughtful pause, he added. 'We must go. Thanks again. We should catch up outside of work sometime.'

'That would be nice', replied Tilly. 'I'll send the formal report by email later.'

But Jamieson and Evason were already halfway down the corridor. Next stop was Akley Football Club, about a mile or so down the road.

Chapter Five

Thursday 12th November – 11:20

The rain had not abated one iota when Jamieson pulled into the car park of Akley FC.

They had passed under a sign which read 'Welcome to Akley FC. Established 1972. Proudly sponsored by Macklin Construction.'

Jamieson got as close to the clubhouse's entrance as he could manage. He had a golf umbrella in the boot of his car. Still, he figured that in the time he had made it to the boot and got the thing up, both he and Evason could have made the twenty-metre dash to the relative dry of the clubhouse awning without getting too soaked.

He was wrong.

Three steps in, he ran into a giant puddle that he hadn't seen, which covered a pothole in the unmade-up surface of the car park. Rainwater seeped into his shoe and shot up his right trouser leg. When he made it to the awning, Evason was there waiting for him. He was sure she had a smirk when she asked: 'Everything ok, Sir?' She, he noticed, did not appear to be at all damp.

The clubhouse reflected the car park. It was tidy and well looked after, but at that same time, there was a tiredness about it. Perhaps the committee should approach their sponsors for some investment.

Once inside, there were changing facilities for home and away teams off to the left, and a smaller changing area for the officials tucked in between. To the right, there was a kitchen and dining area for post-match meals and straight ahead through some double doors was the bar. This was where they headed.

There was a woman behind the bar who was methodically drying pint glasses with a tea towel.

'Good morning,' said Jamieson, brandishing his police warrant card, 'we'd like to talk to someone about one of your players, if possible.'

The woman continued drying the glass: 'That'll be young Ashley James then', she finally said.

Jamieson didn't respond to the comment but merely said, 'Anyone about?'

Still, the woman continued drying the same glass. Then, at last, she lifted her chin and gestured toward the big window which overlooked the pitch: 'That daft bugger out there is probably your best bet.'

Jamieson turned and peered out of the window. It was difficult to see much initially. The window was protected by a wire screen, probably as a result of too many misplaced shots smashing the window too many times, and the constant rain gave a hazy, almost smoky effect on anything beyond.

Finally, he made out a figure pushing a line-marking machine around the edge of the pitch.

He looked back to the woman, who it seemed was finally satisfied with the glass she had been working on and had picked up another: 'Wasting his time.' Then, she said, 'There's supposed to be a reserve game on tonight, but I've told him it'll be cancelled as a mark of respect - only proper. Anyway, if it weren't that, it would be the rain - there's puddles forming on the pitch.'

'Who is it?' Jamieson asked.

'Davey Mcniven' came the reply. 'He does most things round here.'

'How do I get out there?' said Jamieson. Again, the chin gesture, this time towards a door to the
right of the window.'

'Thanks.' And then to Evason, 'You wait here. No point in us both getting soaked.'

Evason watched out of the window as Jamieson made his way pitch side. She could just about make out his mouth moving, but the figure was on the far side and clearly couldn't hear. So, Jamieson had set out across the pitch to get his attention. Finally, with Jamieson halfway across, the figure looked up and jogged towards him. After a brief conversation and the figure pointed back towards the clubhouse, and both he and Jamieson started to return.

Jamieson was truly soaked through.

As they entered through the door, Evason heard Mcniven say, 'It's funny because Debbie behind the bar usually calls me on the mobile if she needs me. It would've saved you getting wet.' There was not a flicker on the glass washer's face as she moved on to the next glass.

'We'll talk in the Manager's office.' Said Mcniven, then almost whispering, 'it's a bit more private in there. This way.'

They followed Mcniven out of the bar and into the home team's changing room. 'The office is at the back of the changing room.' He explained.

They were hit with the heady mix of Deep Heat, male sweat and Paco Rabanne as they went through the door. Jamieson wondered whether Evason had ever encountered such a smell in her life. This time, the look of distaste on her face made him smirk.

The Manager's office didn't smell much better - you could add mustiness to the mix - the room was cramped and stuffed with various paperwork. Framed photographs of past and present players adorned the walls. A bookshelf carried books about various techniques for becoming a better manager. Jamieson felt that Mcniven was at one in here.

They all sat down, Mcniven in the big Manager's chair behind the desk and Jamieson and Evason in smaller chairs facing him.

'Thanks for seeing us, Mr Mcniven; we've been told that you're probably the person we should be talking to', began Jamieson.

'Well, yes, I suppose. I've been with the club for over twenty years now. There's not much happens here that doesn't cross my path in some way.' Said Mcniven. 'Thankfully, not too much like last night's news. Awful, just awful.'

'How did you hear about what had happened?'

'I was here. Helping out in the bar just before my night shift at the supermarket begins at half past ten. One of the lads came in. He was as white as a sheet. He said his girlfriend was a nurse at the local A&E. She'd phoned him at about half eight, nine and told him they'd just bought Ash in. He'd been stabbed, and they couldn't save him. He was dead.'

'What did you do then?' asked Jamieson.

'I think I stayed for about ten minutes. Then I drove home to get ready for work, but by the time I got there, I felt awful, maybe shock, I don't know. So, I called work and said I wouldn't be in for a while and just sat in my kitchen flat with the light turned out. I must've dropped off because I woke up around two and felt better then, so I went to work. Finished at seven, back home for some breakfast and then here to prepare for tonight's game.'

Jamieson nodded: 'How well do you know Jason James? We're not sure he's been made aware of what has happened yet, and we understand you may have his telephone number.'

'Jayce knows. He called me early this morning. Said he'd seen something on Facebook. We go way back, me and Jayce. I thought about phoning him last night but didn't know what to say. How do you tell one of your best mates that his boy's dead? Anyway, I told him what I knew. He was devastated, crying down the phone; it was horrible. He said he'd get the first available flight into Luton. He texted me the flight details earlier on, and I'll go and pick him up. It lands at two thirty.'

Jamieson checked his watch. It was nearly twelve, so Jason James would be at the airport. No point in calling him now if he knows. Let him get over here and start to deal with his grief. They could catch up with him tomorrow.

'I'd like to catch up with Jason. No hurry; when he's ready, if you could let him know.' Said Jamieson: 'Tell me about Ashley.'

'Lovely kid. Special, special footballer. He was going to sign professionally for a big club. I'll tell you, for a small local club, we've had our share of kids who have gone on to play at a high level, you know, professionally in the lower leagues. We've had a couple who have had spells with Premier League sides, and we even had one lad who made the bench for England in a friendly, didn't get on the pitch though, shame.'

'But Ash. Well, Ash was in a different class. He had everything - touch, poise, anticipation, strength - it was like he was born with a ball tied to his right foot. At thirteen, he was playing for our under-seventeen side. At fourteen, he was in the reserve side. The under seventeens christened him 'Baby Ronaldo', so the reserves went and called him 'Baby Messi'. And he was a great kid, kind, polite, looked out for his brother and sisters.'

'Did he ever play for the first team here?' Asked Jamieson.

'No. League rules, you had to be seventeen to play in the first team. Makes a lot of sense that does. Some of the older opponents would snap a youngster in two as much as look at them. So, it was a protective thing as much as anything.'

Jamieson nodded: 'These days, ' he began ', you hear of kids signing for professional clubs from the age of, what, six? Eight? Why didn't that happen here?'

Mcniven took a deep breath in: 'That was Jayce. Jayce was a good player, not as good as Ash, but top drawer, nonetheless. When he was eleven he got signed on by a mid-table Premier League club, they've dropped a few divisions since mind. I think his parents got a couple of hundred quid a month to cover expenses and that, but it was made clear to them and Jayce that he couldn't play for anyone other than them. That meant no Akley FC couldn't even train with his mates on a Wednesday or have a kick-about in the local park. That hurt him a lot, even though he could see the bigger picture. He stayed with that club year after year. He's not a big lad; you'll see that when you meet him, and he was always worried each year that he hadn't grown as much as some of the others, but the club said to him, 'don't worry if you're good enough, you're big enough'. That's what they said year after year after year. And he believed them.'

Mcniven tutted: 'Then just before his sixteenth birthday him and his parents were called in; they thought to sign his first professional contract, and everyone was so excited for Jayce. But the club dropped the bombshell, 'decided against offering a contract', 'there are other clubs', 'circulate your name and skillset to other clubs', 'don't be downhearted."

"Don't be downhearted'? Well, he was devastated.'

'And he didn't want that for Ash?' said Jamieson.

'No, course not, why would you? Difference was that he could tell that it would be different with Ash. The kid was developing at eleven, physically and skill-wise; there were already clubs sniffing around. But Jayce wanted the lad to develop mentally as well. He wanted him to be around his mates, to grow up playing football in a team full of his mates and not in a group thrown together by a professional club. So, they sat down and decided he wouldn't sign pro until his seventeenth birthday. Even his ex-missus, Holly, was on board with that.' Mcniven spread his hands in front of him in a resigned way. 'And now......'

'Did you ever have any trouble with Ash? You know, serious stuff, not the occasional scrap between mates.' asked Jamieson.

Mcniven paused for a moment. 'At this club, we're big on a level of discipline. As you say, occasional scraps between mates are a given as long as it's not a regular occurrence. But anything considered more serious, and we operate a three-strikes rule, so effectively two warnings, transgress again, and you're on your way. We're rigid with this rule and over the years we have lost some gifted footballers who haven't been able to adhere to our rules.'

'About this time last year, Ash fell in with a slightly older boy. A lad called Michael Macklin. Between you and I, Macklin wasn't a good player; he was physically big but not up to much. He was taken on as a favour to our sponsor; it was his son. The Dad could see that the kid was going off the rails and thought that an interest in football would take the edge off, as it were. It didn't. Michael was always the one with the new boots, new trainers, new tracksuit, and latest phone telling other kids that their kit was crap and that he could have a word with his Dad and have them thrown off the team, all of that sort of stuff. Anyway, he didn't last long. He was soon on two strikes, and then the third was a serious one, reports that he'd been hanging around with gangs, drugs, etc. He didn't deny it when we confronted him. He knew what was coming and got in first, said we were a shit football club, and he had better things to be doing.'

'And Ash?' asked Jamieson.

'We'll, although nothing ever stuck, there were some rumours and murmurings that through Macklin, Ash was involved with these gangs as well. Now he was a smart kid, so if he was, you wouldn't find out about it easily. But it just wouldn't go away. Still hasn't to this day, in fact. Anyway, nothing concrete, just rumour.'

Jamieson nodded thoughtfully; "Thank you, Mr Mcniven, you've been very helpful. We may come back and ask some more questions, but it's early days, and we're still trying to get as many pieces of the puzzle together as possible. If you could let Jason James know that we would like to catch up with him, that would be helpful, and if you have his number, perhaps you could give it to DS Evason here.'

Mcniven found the number on his mobile and scribbled it onto a scrap of paper for Evason.

Under the awning outside, Jamieson said to Evason, 'Do we know anyone in the gangs unit who could help us?'

Evason nodded: 'I know a couple of names we could try.' She replied.

And with that, they were back out into the ever-pouring rain, racing back to the car. Although this time, Jamieson avoided the deep puddle he found on the way in, which would inevitably mean throwing away his favourite pair of now ruined brogues.

Chapter Six

Thursday 12th November – 12:10

Roger Johnson was gay; he was also a policeman; he played rugby; he instinctively knew that he would meet Someone who he could love both physically and spiritually and that that person would reciprocate that love unconditionally; he wanted to get married (he was a traditionalist) and for that day alone he wanted to be the centre of attention; he wanted to be a Father; he loved Chinese food but if pushed would opt for Indian; he loved The Simpsons, at least the earlier series, of late the producers had made Homer less of a bigot and he couldn't understand why, when America and the rest of the world were becoming more bigoted, a decision had been made to make America's second favourite bigot, less bigoted; he was loyal to a fault; and many, many, more things that made up Roger Johnson.

Individually, none of these traits defined him. Collectively they all did.

Occasionally, only very occasionally, he found it irksome that the first trait in his list - his sexuality - was of more interest to society than, say, his love of The Simpsons. It rankled that the rating attributed to who he loved carried more weight than so many other, more interesting aspects of who he was.

He wasn't sure if he was 'out'. He hadn't taken to Facebook to proclaim that he was 'queer and here'. But, at the same time, he hadn't announced that he was a policeman who was 'proper to be a copper' or a fan of Indian cuisine who sought 'glory in a tandoori'.

His family were aware.

His Mum and Dad were old school, and his brother was the straightest man you could ever find. As one of his friends pointed out, it wasn't his fault; it was just the way he wore his genes.

Johnson had corralled his family into the living room one Sunday after lunch and told them: 'I'm gay.' That was what he said, 'I'm gay.'

'Jesus', said his Mother ', I know that. I thought you were going to tell us that you had cancer.'

His Dad stood up: 'Are you happy, son?' When Johnson said 'yes', his Dad shook him by the hand and said, 'then that's good enough for me.'

His brother grinned. 'So, you're a gay, rugby-playing policeman. I can live with that.' And he opened his arms and hugged him. That meant so much coming from the straightest man in the world.

Johnson's brother, Steve, was a football-playing solicitor. He did a lot of legal aid work for people who had been arrested and couldn't afford legal representation. His stock entry into all Birthday and Christmas cards to Johnson was, 'You lock them up, Bro, and I'll get them out!'

Johnson wasn't aware whether the people he worked with had any idea about his private life. He thought: Stone, probably not. Evason, probably. Jamieson, who knew, the important thing was that he wouldn't care, so long as Johnson did a good job, which, Johnson thought, I do.

But, at this moment, all this paled into insignificance as Johnson sat in awe of the fifty-something, slightly crumpled man sitting next to him and driving them to the local Social Services office.

'So, Sandy,' he asked, 'When you walked into that school this morning, you had no idea you would be addressing over three hundred kids?'

'No'

'And you'd had no preparation?'

'No'

'And you've never done it before?'

'No'

'Well, I have to say, mate, that was one of the most astonishing things I have ever witnessed.'

And he was right; it was. With no preparation and no real idea of what he would say, DS Peter Stone addressed his audience of grieving teenagers. Everything he said was right. Every pause spot on. Every gesture held their attention. He spoke for ten minutes, told them it was ok to be sad, that it was ok to cry, told them that the teachers were going through the same emotions as they were and that if any of them needed to speak, then their teachers would listen, that their teachers would find people who were trained to listen. No one should suffer this in silence; that grief was better shared.

In short, he was awesome.

Not one for fanfare, Stone merely said: 'Someone had to step up. Some of those teachers are barely out of school themselves. There's a lot of healing that needs to happen in that school, and I hope the bloody authorities understand that and give them proper support.'

And those were his closing words on the subject.

The offices of social services were drab beyond belief. It was well known that a distinct lack of funding was available, which clearly stretched to the upkeep of council premises.

Stone swung into the crowded car park and squeezed into the only spare space next to a thoughtless individual who had ignored the parking bay lines. The rain continued as they scampered across the car park and up to the entrance.

They made their way through the doors and up to the front desk. Stone checked his watch: 'Detectives Stone and Johnson to see case worker Rees-Smith at twelve o'clock. I apologise that we are ten minutes late.'

The receptionist smiled: 'No problem, gentlemen. Take a seat, and I'll let Eileen know you're here.'

No sooner had they settled into the beaten-up sofa than a middle-aged woman approached them with an outstretched hand: 'Detectives', she said, shaking their hands in turn, 'Let's go into the board room where there's a bit more space.'

The board room was a stretch, thought Stone, as they entered what was little more than a glorified cupboard with an oversized table crammed into the centre.

They settled, and Eileen opened a file that was on the table in front of her.

'So,' she began, 'the Matthews family, Holly and her four children, what can I help you with?'

'Balls', thought Stone '. She's not been made aware of why we're here. This will be a difficult start to the meeting. Depending on her reaction, it may end before it even begins.'

Johnson stepped in. He felt that Stone had done his share of the heavy lifting for the day. 'I'm sorry to be the one to tell you, but the eldest son, Ashley, was stabbed last night. He passed away at Luton General around eight-thirty.'

Eileen's mouth dropped: 'Good God. That's a shock. Given everything that was going on around him, he was an incredibly well-adjusted individual. Do you know what happened?'

'Investigation pending, I'm afraid. We're just trying to put things together.'

'Well, whatever I can help you with. I've been their case manager for the last fifteen years.'

'Thanks', said Johnson. 'Perhaps we can start with some family background.'

'Of course, Of course', said Eileen sifting through the file and pulling out a handwritten family tree. 'So Mum is Holly Matthews, born 1982. Ashley was the eldest. He was born in 2001. Dad is Jason James. He and Holly split up in 2003. Jason lives in Spain but was a very hands-on father to Ashley. Then comes Lewis, born in 2003. Father unknown and the birth certificate was left blank; however, it was definitely not Jason James, the reason that he and Holly split up in 2003. Then come Anneka and Aimee, born in 2007 and 2009, respectively. Their father is Bobby Hill. He's an older man born in 1970. He was not the best father in the world, but he is by no means the worst either. His income is limited, and whilst some gets through to his daughters, quite a lot is spent in various pubs in and around the area.'

She ran her eyes over the piece of paper, satisfied that there was nothing confidential, she went off to make a copy that Stone and Johnson could take with them.

When she returned, Stone picked up: 'So what was family life like?' He asked.

'Well, Holly is an addict and bipolar, a potent mix, first diagnosed when she was sixteen. That's when we got involved. I don't think that family life was all that sweet. Then she met Jason James, and he was very good for her. He looked after her and kept her addictions under control. Ash was born, and Holly was a good mother,; things were good for a year or so. Then Jason had an offer to work in Spain for some football team. It was an excellent opportunity. He wanted Holly and Ashley to join him out there, you know, make a brand-new start. But her mother, the redoubtable Mrs Matthews, wouldn't have it. 'You can't take my daughter and grandson away from me' sort of thing, not she'd had seen them much in the previous six months - forget I said that please - anyway Jason went to Spain and arranged with his new employer that he could come back every fourth week, schedule allowing, and for important and family occasions. Very good of them, I think.'

Eileen took a sip of water from a bottle she had brought in with her before continuing: 'Anyway, without Jason around for a lot of the time, Holly slipped back into her bad ways. Any money Jason would send home, and he was on a decent wage, seemed to disappear on booze and drugs. Then Holly fell pregnant, and we all thought she might revert to being a good mother again, but as soon as the baby was born, there was a problem.'

'Jason wanted a paternity test?' said Stone.

Eileen looked up. 'Have you met Jason?' she asked. Stone shook his head.

'He didn't need a paternity test. Jason is a black man, and Lewis was clearly a white baby.'

'Well, Jason tried to see past Holly's infidelity, but loyalty runs deep within that family. In the end, he'll be the first to admit he couldn't deal with the betrayal. He left her. He still came back to see Ash on the same terms as before, but instead of staying with Holly, he'd stay at his Mum's place. He still sent money back; in fact, he increased what he sent. He didn't know if Lewis' father was making any provision for his son, and at the end of the day, it wasn't the child's fault that everything was so messed up, so why should he suffer.'

'I'm not sure whether Holly ever disclosed who Lewis' father was, not to Jason, not to anyone.'

Eileen rubbed her hands together and puffed out her cheeks. She continued talking: 'Holly lurched along, really. The kids were always well looked after, so there were no real concerns there. Despite her being such a ghastly individual, Holly's mother always made sure that the kids were looked after. Then Holly bumped into Bobby Hill. Seemed inevitable in the end, I guess, they moved in similar circles, and it was only probably a matter of time before they would get together. Bobby's not a bad man, but ,he was no Jason for Holly. Suddenly before you could blink, there were two more mouths to feed. The income that was coming in, Bobby's salary and benefits and what Jason was sending, were insufficient to run a household of six and provide for two addicts' requirements.'

'Around this time last year, things really came to a head. The rent had always been paid in dribs and drabs - that's an old trick, even if you can't afford all this month's rent, pay something - then when it came to potential eviction, it would always be viewed positively, at least there had been some effort to cover the rent, and it could buy some time.'

'Unfortunately, Holly and Bobby had not paid any rent for more than nine months and were six and a half thousand in arrears. Letters and court orders were ignored. Eventually, bailiffs turned up. Bobby scarpered, and moved away, nature of the beast, I'm afraid. The bailiffs gave them a final date of one month until eviction and a leaflet that outlined an appeal process. All this was played out in front of the neighbours and, worse still, in front of the kids.'

It was Stone's turn to sigh: 'Christ. So where are they living now?'

Eileen picked up the phone on the desk: 'Bear with me for one moment.' She jabbed in a short number: 'Hello Martha. Can you do a check for me, please? Yes, it's 112672.' She listened intently and made a few notes on her pad. Then she put the receiver down again.

She looked at Stone and shrugged: 'That's just it. They're living in the same place. The eviction never happened. Perhaps with some help, Holly went through the appeal process, and the eviction was postponed. Current rent is fully up to date, and the arrears are down to.....,' she checked her pad; '....£1200. Something, somewhere, changed, and we're not sure what. I make monthly visits to see how things are. Holly seems to be zoned out a lot of the time, but her mother is always there, usually with Ashley. The kids seem fine, and any questions are fielded in a tight-lipped fashion. There's a united front; you know: 'we're fine, we're getting there, leave us alone."

Stone slowly nodded his head: 'No clue?' He asked. 'Jason, maybe?'

Eileen replied and pulled a face: 'I don't think so. He still sends money, but he's got his own family now in Spain.'

Stone puffed out his cheeks: 'That's probably enough for us to be going on with now. You've been most helpful. Thanks for your time.'

He glanced down at the family tree she had given him earlier and pointed at Holly's name: 'What does this mean? Next to Holly's name, TW circled.'

For the first time, Eileen looked flustered: 'Oh, I must have drawn that chart over five years ago and was just doodling as I went.' Then, she paused: 'It means I thought Holly was a train wreck; sorry, very unprofessional of me.'

Stone stood up to leave; Johnson followed. They both shook Eileen's hand and thanked her again. Then, as they left the building, Stone turned to Johnson: 'She's not wrong, very unprofessional, but it does give us a strong pointer to exactly what we are dealing with.'

Chapter Seven

Thursday 12th November – 15:15

Driving back to the station, Stone phoned Jamieson.

'Just on our way back now', said Jamieson

'Us too,' said Stone. 'Your ETA?'

'Twenty minutes.'

'We're about ten', said Stone 'it looks like the Giorgio's are on us. The usual for you both?'

Affirmative grunts. 'See you soon.' said Stone and hung up.

Stone peered through the windscreen. Even with the wipers at full speed, the pouring rain made it very difficult to see, and for once, Stone stayed well within the speed limit.

'What are your thoughts so far, Rog?' asked Stone.

Johnson thought: 'Well, I'd be interested in what the others have found out today, but it increasingly feels to me like there is some element of gang and drugs going on. Where have the family found the best part of twelve grand in the last year to turn their situation around? It just doesn't add up.'

Stone turned into the car park and pulled up. He gave Johnson a ten-pound note. 'For the coffees.' He said.

'Four cups.' Protested Johnson. 'We'll need four hands.'

'Nah', said Stone. 'Get one of them cardboard things you can fit four cups into. Try not to spill too much.' He grinned.

Johnson leapt out and hustled down towards the cafe, avoiding puddles on the way.

Lately, Stone had met with Margaret several times, and it became clearer that the marriage was over. He didn't get the impression that Margaret's male friend was any more than an acquaintance and that she was just living there to give her some space. However, Margaret's conversations were more about moving forwards, and it sounded like she meant separately. On a couple of occasions, she mentioned testing the water by putting their house on the market and seeing what interest they got.

Stone was afraid to ask the outright question, and it seemed that Margaret felt the same about saying what she actually wanted. It all added up to a strange impasse. They were going nowhere pretty slowly.

Unfortunately, the second time they met, Stone hadn't been selective enough about where. In the shadows of the pub sat one of the biggest busybodies in Bedfordshire Constabulary. As Stone and Margaret got up to leave, the busybody caught his eye and smiled a smile that said, 'you've been caught out, boy.'

Hence the whispering campaign going around the station that Stone and his wife were back together. It just wasn't true, and he was a bit fed up with it.

Back in the office, the team was reunited, and coffee'd up. Two trips to Giorgio's in one day sounded extravagant, but, except for Evason, they had all had their turn being soaked today. The coffee helped to smooth that frustration out.

Jamieson began, with Evason chipping in where necessary. He talked about Holly and her Mother. On the journey back, Evason had ascertained from Crime Scene Manager Lisa Wooster that neither Holly's mobile nor the weapon had yet to be located. The door-to-door officers had found some footage from the doorbell cameras. Wooster said it was very grainy. Some figures could have been Ashley and Holly passing around the time Holly had said. However, 'could have' was the best she could offer.

Jamieson moved on to the brief visit to Tilly Jenner, the Pathologist, and that the weapon was more likely to be a common kitchen knife rather than the gang-favoured zombie knife. Jamieson also remarked how Dr Jenner had said it was 'incredibly unlucky' that the femoral artery was struck in the manner that it was.

Johnson said, 'Does this mean that it could have been unintentional then? Not so much the attack, moreover the fact that Ashley died.'

'Good point.' said Jamieson. 'Although the Crown Prosecution Service will determine that. Our initial job is to find out what happened, from there, decisions around intent can be made. If you leave home with a weapon, there has to be an element of intention to use it; otherwise, why take it with you? I'm not sure I buy that having a knife offers some defence or protection. Anyway, I digress........'

'We then met up with David Mcniven at Akley Football Club. It seems that Ashley was an incredibly talented footballer, and that was his calling. He would have turned seventeen soon, and there were several clubs, the big boys, vying for his signature. A potential name of interest is Michael Macklin, who was at the club at the same time and had links to gangs. We'll need to follow that up. Also, Ashley's father, Jason James is aware and is travelling over from Spain if he hasn't already landed. We will need to speak to him at some point.'

Stone picked up and gave an outline of the meeting with Helen Miller. He eyed Johnson as if to dare him to mention Stone's performance at the assembly - he didn't want the fuss. However, he did highlight that although Helen Miller didn't think that Ashley would have been involved in gangs and drugs, she described him as loyal and would do 'anything' he needed to do for the better of his family. Make what you will of that.

Johnson continued. He outlined the meeting with social services, particularly the rent arrears, which have been cleared over the last twelve months from who knows where. That would be one for Holly Matthews at some future point.

'Ok', Jamieson started summing up ', Progress. I think we have a better picture of things.'

'Tomorrow we've got a meeting with.....?' He looked at Evason.

'Detective Inspector Gary Moses from the gangs unit at nine fifteen.'

Jamieson pondered: 'Sandy, why don't you join me for that one?'

Stone nodded. Evason looked a little peeved; after all, she had set up the meeting.

'Claire and Rog, why don't you do some digging around Michael Macklin and the company his father runs, was it Macklin Construction? Rog, see if you can find the journalist who wrote that piece in the local paper that you mentioned. There might be some mileage there. Perhaps touch base with the door-to-door team and Lisa Wooster's lot, and see if anything else has turned up. Claire, we've not been asked yet, but please consider whether a press conference would be of any value, you know, it might jog someone, somewhere's memory.'

'Ok, until tomorrow then. Everyone have a good evening.'

On the way home, Jamieson made two calls and received one.

The first call was to Lucy: 'Hi, I'm on my way home.'

'Great. I'll sort some dinner out.' Replied Lucy.

'Shall I stop off and pick something up?' He asked hopefully.

He could hear cupboards being opened and closed: 'No need. I've got some pasta, and I'll knock up a tomato sauce - easy.'

Jamieson adored his wife, and he knew she absolutely understood ninety-nine per cent of what he was all about. Still, she did not get his love of takeaway food or his complete lack of any kind of enthusiasm for any kind of pasta with any kind of tomato sauce.

Lucy knew Jamieson adored her - she knew she was lucky - and she absolutely understood him one hundred per cent. She knew he loved takeaway food, but she also knew that he was approaching that age where your body could not break down fatty foods in the same way. Additionally, Jamieson's father had suffered his first heart attack at a similar age, so whenever Jamieson offered to pick something up on the way home, she would always steer him away and down the pasta route, bang a few cupboard doors - there was even one time when she didn't have any pasta in the cupboard and had to run next door to borrow some spaghetti. He may be a successful detective, but he hadn't worked this one out yet!

The next call was to Jason James. Jamieson wondered whether speaking to the grieving father was too early but decided he would do so anyway. Evason had entered James' number into his phone, so Jamieson scrolled until he found it. He pressed 'call'.

The phone was answered almost immediately: 'Jason James.'

'Hello, Mr James. My name is Detective Inspector Alex Jamieson. David Mcniven gave me your number. I wonder if you have a moment?'

'Davey did mention it. What can I do to help?'

'Firstly, I am sorry about Ashley.'

'You and me both, said James

'Mr James, I'd like to catch up with you to discuss things. I'm desperate to get to the bottom of this for everyone's, especially Ashley's sake.'

James thought: 'I'll tell you what. There's a reserve team match at Akley tomorrow evening, seven thirty kick-off. I'll be here watching; football is my form of escapism; it's how I get away from it all if you're up for it. I'll stand you a half-time, Bovril.'

'Ok. Sounds good. I may be a little late. How will I find you?

'Well, it's not Old Trafford, and if this rain keeps up, the usual crowd of 50 will be even smaller. So you'll find me alright.'

'Ok,' said Jamieson: 'I'll see you tomorrow.'

'One last thing', said James. 'Call me Jason, Jayce or JJ but not Mr James; that's my old man.'

'Fine,' said Jamieson ', in that case, I'm Alex.'

The last call was incoming and came from Billy Watson, Alex's oldest and closest friend. Many moons ago, Billy and Alex had formed a band called the Wailing Bunnies. Little did they realise that that same band would still be going some thirty years later - almost entirely through Billy's efforts.

The Wailing Bunnies had built a solid local reputation as the 'go-to' covers band. However, Billy was keen to keep them current, so they covered most basics - Weddings, Anniversaries, 60th, 70th and 80th Birthday parties, 18th Birthday parties, School proms and even the occasional Bar Mitzvah.

This meant they rehearsed hard - Billy had them together at least twice a month. He supplemented his income by offering guitar lessons and hiring himself out as a reliable session musician - his guitar playing was excellent. As a backing singer, he offered something a little more than today's auto-tuned stars.

'Just reminding you about 11th December', said Billy

'11th December, ' repeated Jamieson, not a clue.

'That is the date of this year's fundraiser at the Bell. And I want you there.' Although not an active band member, Billy has always maintained that there would always be space on stage for his best mate and band co-founder.

'And,' continued Billy. 'I want to see all the people that you work with there. And Lucy. And Xander. And Jus. And all their mates. Twenty quid a ticket includes a buffet - an absolute steal.'

Earlier this year, Billy had lost his Mum, Dolly, following a particularly harrowing battle against dementia. This year's beneficiaries were the Alzheimer's Society, and Billy wanted to top £10,000 in the name of Dolly. And when Billy wanted something, he usually got his way.

'As it's so close to Christmas, I want to introduce a couple of Festive numbers into the set. Liz singing 'All I want for Christmas is you' - who needs Mariah Carey? - that Slade thing and the one Springsteen does, you know 'you'd better watch out, you'd better not cry', that one.' Liz Willis was the long-standing female vocalist with the band, and when Billy said, 'Who needs Mariah Carey?' He wasn't far off - she had a better voice than most professional singers. It would be nice if Mariah made an appearance, though it would sell a few more tickets.

'Ok', said Jamieson. 'Please text Lucy, though; she'll stick it in the communal diary.'

'Will do', said Billy. They chatted for a further ten minutes about everything and nothing before Billy signed off. He had a student due in ten minutes and had to prepare. 'Twenty-six-year-old blonde,' was all he'd say.

Later, at home, with the pasta eaten and the dishwater stacked, Jamieson and Lucy sat in the living room. Jamieson tried to relax but was suddenly overcome with emotion.

Lucy picked up on it: 'What's up?' she asked.

'Ah, I dunno', sighed Jamieson 'it's always the same with this job. You spend so much time the first twenty-four hours trying to gather information and work out what has happened that you can lose sight of the victim in all this.' He looked at his watch. 'Just over twenty-four hours ago, this young kid left his house for the last time. He almost literally had the world at his feet, and then an injudicious swipe of a knife, and it's all over; everything has gone, and everything has changed for the people who loved him,. Nothing is the same. He becomes another statistic. And no matter what I do or find out, that's what he'll be - a statistic.'

'Not to his family, he won't.' said Lucy. 'He'll be loved and remembered forever. And you do what you do to prevent things like this from happening in the future. For him and his family, you and your team will do your utmost to provide answers as to who, what and why, and you do it professionally and sensitively.'

'But you also do it for future Ashleys and their families, and if you save one life or prevent one young lad from making the wrong decision in the future, then it's all been worth it.'

She crossed the room and hugged him.

Once again, she was right. Once again, she had nailed it.

Chapter Eight

Friday 13th November – 08:20

Jamieson knew that he had pissed Evason off yesterday when he suggested that Stone accompany him to the gang's unit instead of her. She was the more obvious choice, but Jamieson would deal with that later.

Jamieson had heard the rumours about Stone and Margaret like almost everyone else in the station, and he wanted to understand the current situation. Although, first and foremost, Stone was a work colleague, Jamieson and he had been working together for nearly four years, extending the relationship from work colleague towards friendship. So, it was as a friend that Jamieson spoke to Stone on the twenty-minute journey to the building, which amongst other things, housed the gang's unit.

'How're things between you and Margaret now, Pete?'

'Ah,' said Stone ', You've been caught up with the old rumour mill, Alex.'

'Yes and No, actually.' Replied Jamieson. 'Lucy asked, was the main reason for me asking.' She hadn't. Her opinion was it was no one else's business and that the two of them should sort it out for themselves.

"Well, I don't think it's going to happen, is the short answer. We're close to putting the house on the market as part of the great divvy up.'

'That's too bad', said Jamieson: 'Twenty-five years is a long time.'

'Twenty-seven.' Stone corrected him, 'but we had a good run, we had some really good times, and you grow apart, I guess. The house sale should bring in enough for each of us to get something nice, smaller, but still nice enough. Margaret thinks she might move back up to Nottingham to be nearer her Mum and Dad, which makes sense; they're both pushing eighty now. We're on cordial enough terms, so she'll leave me with my police pension, and I'll leave her with her teaching pension.

'What about the bloke she moved in with?' Said Jamieson, risking a short response.

"I think he was keener than her. Although, to be honest with you, she may have used the situation to her advantage. You know, a roof over her head and all that.'

'Can I say,' said Jamieson 'that this was not how I thought this conversation would go. I honestly thought you'd say that everything was patched up and things would go on as before.'

Stone made a noncommittal grunt.

'How do you feel about it all?'

'Honestly', said Stone ', I'm alright. Margaret was right. We have grown apart; we have different interests. My work has become all important to me and, you'll know this, it's not nine to five. And at home, I'm always thinking about whatever case we're working on. I can't, or maybe, won't, switch off. It sounds corny, but people rely on us; they need us. Who knows, when I'm on my own, I might get my fishing rods or golf clubs out again. Start trying to find a better balance.'

This time it was Jamieson who was noncommittal - he knew that with Stone and his police work, it was all or nothing.

The rest of the journey went quickly and was uneventful. Eventually, they arrived at a modern building that housed many businesses and organisations, including the gang unit. This was moving towards modern policing and away from the old custom-built police stations, whereas many police units were crammed in as possible. Here the gangs unit would have a short lease on either a floor or a suite of offices, and the situation would be reviewed every two or three years. As they entered the foyer, Jamieson read the list of organisations sharing the building. There were IT companies, recruitment agencies, and laboratories, and there was the gang unit on floor four.

They took the lift to the fourth floor.

The unit was right opposite the lift, and Stone pressed the entry buzzer. A bright voice quickly answered: 'Hello?'

Stone spoke: 'DI Jamieson and DS Stone for DI Moses.'

'Be right with you. Can you have your warrant cards to hand, please' said the voice.

Within seconds the door opened with a buzz, and a young woman wearing jeans and a T-shirt stood in front of them. They showed her their identification, and she ushered them in.

'Morning', she said. 'My name is Lily. Hess has been held up. He's giving a talk at the local school..' Stone shivered involuntarily. 'He's running about fifteen minutes late, so Hess asked me to look after you.'

'Hess?' said Jamieson

'Sorry, force of habit, DI Moses. He's known as Hess around here. Can I get you a coffee?'

There had been no time for a Giorgio's this morning, but neither Jamieson nor Stone felt ready for Bedford Police Force's finest sludge just yet.

"The building has Costa machine on the next floor up,' offered Lily.

Jamieson and Stone looked at each other. Jamieson raised his eyebrows: "Well, in that case, I'd like a large Americano with milk, please.'

'Two of those, please', said Stone. 'What do we owe you?'

'Oh, nothing', said Lily. Then she frowned. 'I think the cost is included in the monthly rent. I'll be five minutes.' And she disappeared.

Stone smiled. 'How the other half live, eh?'

When she returned with the coffees, Jamieson asked her her role within the unit.

'Actually, I'm on a year's placement from Cardiff University. This is my third year of four of a phycology degree. I'm interested in the phycology of gangs, so when this placement came through, I thought, 'why not?'. I live reasonably locally and am in the office two days a week. The other three days, I work from home.'

'Sounds great', said Jamieson. 'So why don't you share some of your ideas about gangs with a couple of old-school coppers?' He grinned as he said it to put the girl more at ease.

'Well, ok,' she said, 'But remember these are my ideas, so if someone more experienced like Hess comes in and says that I'm talking rubbish, then go with him and not me.'

'I'm sure he won't', said Jamieson smiling.

'So, there are many different categories of gangs, but I prefer to simplify it into two - I see functional and dysfunctional gangs,' began Lily.

'So, let's start with dysfunctional because it's easier. A dysfunctional gang has an end goal but no real strategy for getting there. So, they want to make money but have no real plan as to how to do it. Usually, they sell drugs but have no regular supplier, and they shop around for the cheapest deal, so there's no loyalty. When there is a shortage of a particular drug, the supplier will supply their loyal customers first, so the dysfunctional gang misses out. Leadership is an issue. There are usually too many egos and, no defined chain of command. Conflicting decisions are made, and because there is no defined plan or chain of command, there's no focus on activity.

Another leadership issue surrounds keeping the younger gang members in line. With weak leadership, when a gang member is 'dissed', the immediate reaction from those gang members down the line is revenge of a physical nature. That is, they put the word out that they are looking for whoever has 'dissed' them and when word gets back with their whereabouts, everyone piles in a car, finds them and dishes out their form of revenge, which normally involves a knife and frequently a death. That's when you watch the news and see that five gang members have been jailed for life for being involved in the death of a different gang member. So that takes five of your members out in one fell swoop. How can that be anything but dysfunctional?'

Jamieson nodded: 'and functional?' He asked.

Lily continued: 'Reverse all of the above, really.'

'Functional gangs are almost like a medium-sized business and are often more successful. Of course, they're never going to win a business of the year award, but the model should.'

'They effectively have a CEO and a Board of Directors who make all decisions. They build effective relationships with suppliers, customers and staff and, as importantly, other companies with whom they share synergy. But, of course, the terminology is different; you would swap gang leader for CEO, senior gang members for Board of Directors, suppliers, well, for suppliers, customers for users, staff for junior gang members and other companies for other gangs. Additionally, they build relationships with other stakeholders, but you should ask Hes more about that.' Jamieson swore she had a glint in her eye when she said the last sentence.

'Dissing' is not an issue because it is just name-calling, school playground stuff. If it ever should get out of hand, the heads of each gang involved get together and agree it's not conducive to business, and it's stamped out. What they don't do is rush out and stab the first person they see; it brings unnecessary attention to what they are trying to achieve. The functional gangs prefer to work away from the glare of any spotlight. And frankly, why wouldn't they? It makes their lives so much simpler!'

Jamieson took a mouthful of coffee. 'And where do the police fit into all of this?'

'They facilitate, I guess', said Lily. 'As long as there are people who take drugs, there will be people who supply them—basic supply and demand. People like Hes understand that you'll never eliminate drugs and gang culture entirely, but you can manage it. We hadn't had a gang-related death for two years until the other evening. Before that, it was six in the previous two years. That reduction is down to Hess and the team's work. Working with the gangs for more acceptable outcomes.'

Jamieson was impressed and made a mental note to determine whether his team could offer placements to these bright, young university students. A whole new outlook to local policing. He was just about to ask another question when the buzzer on the entry door sounded, and the door burst open. A big bloke with a laptop bag slung over his shoulder and an umbrella in his hand came in. His raincoat dripped.

He had his head down: 'Still pissing down.' He announced and looked up. 'Oh, sorry!' he said, 'company.'

He stuck out his hand: 'DI Gary Moses. AKA Hess.'

Chapter Nine

Friday 13th November – 09:20

DI Moses, or Hess, as Jamieson had already come to think of him, was a giant of a man. He stood at least six feet six, and if he played rugby, and Jamieson had already decided that he did, he was either a prop or number eight.

Jamieson could also see why he might make an excellent policeman to work in gangs. He gave off a no-fear, no-bullshit vibe, but at the same time, he had a big honest, open kind of face. You would believe what he told you and want to work with him.

He smiled: 'She's impressive, isn't she? Lily? To be honest with you, I've been outside the door for the past ten minutes listening. She does that dysfunctional, functional explanation much better than I ever could.'

'Very', said Jamieson 'how old is she?'

'Twenty, twenty-one early next year

'Will she join the force?'

'If she's got any sense, she'll finish off next year and then do her Masters. Then we'll contract her in at twice the cost. It's how it usually works.' Explained Hess. 'Anyway, gentlemen, Claire said you wanted to talk about gangs. What do you need to know?'

Jamieson picked up: 'Yes. First of all, thanks for your time. Secondly, you may have heard that there was a stabbing a couple of nights ago, a sixteen-year-old on Rankin Avenue at the junction with Holmes Road. One of the avenues we're looking at is gang related.'

'That's a reasonable start', said Hess. 'Let me tell you what I know about that area. Two gangs are based there - L6 and Dons - Rankin Avenue runs East to West. L6 has most of the business north of Rankin Avenue, and Dons, a bigger outfit, has the business to the south, taking in the Holderness housing estate. There is a tacit agreement that both gangs can trade on Rankin Avenue without any interference from the other.'

'Both of these gangs are what Lily would term as functional. There's respect there. In fact, Danny Mack, who runs L6, used to be one of Dons' Captains and board members,' He grinned. 'But respectfully asked that he be allowed to branch off and form his own gang. This was agreed by Antonio, Tony, Di Angelo, who runs Dons. The two gangs are separate entities but coexist because it suits both to do so.'

Hess puffed out his cheeks. 'Now both guys run tight ships; neither has had any trouble involving violence for a long time. I don't think another gang would try to infiltrate their patches. Dons, particularly, command too much respect.....' He looked doubtful: 'What about the lad who died? What do we know about him?'

'Ashley James.' said Stone stepping in. 'We understand from his Mother that he's had a bit of cash of late. She doesn't know where it has come from.'

Hess wrote 'Ashley James' on a pad in front of him: 'Not a name I've come across.' He said.

Jamieson had a thought: 'What about Michael Macklin?' He asked. 'We think he may have got Ashley involved somehow.'

'I've heard of him.' Confirmed Hess. 'He's with Dons. Di Angelo took him on because his old man is in construction, and Di Angelo thought that might be a good contact. He's now regretting it, though, and says that the kid is a liability, a Billy Big Bollocks, can't keep his trap shut, always pushing for more responsibility. I shouldn't say it, but if anyone was going to get stabbed.......' He left the remainder of the sentence unsaid.

" Look, " said Hess, I'm'm meeting with Di Angelo later today. I'll ask him. See if any of his Capos know anything.'

'Capos?' Said Jamieson.

Hess gave a little laugh. 'Yeah. Di Angelo is a massive fan of The Godfather. So, a lot of his language is taken from the film. He doesn't have 'captains' in his gang; he has 'caporegimes', and his Dad, who ran the gang before him and now offers advice, is the 'consigliere', Tom Hagen in the Godfather. Have you seen the film?'

'Oh yes.' Said Jamieson nodding knowingly. 'One of the best. Although Goodfellas is slightly better.'

'You think so?' said Hess, raising his eyebrows. 'Anyway, I'll speak to The Don about it and get back to you.'

'Oh!' Said Jamieson, suddenly remembering, 'Ashley James had two phones on him. One was an iPhone, which has been identified as his personal phone, and the other was probably a cheap phone bought from one of the supermarkets. No messages on the cheap phone. Both are with the Tech team trying to recover calls, text messages, that sort of thing.'

'Sounds like a graft phone, doesn't it' said Hess. 'If your tech boys are struggling to find time to break it down, send it over here, and ours will take a look. If it is a burner, the texts recovered will be addresses for drug deliveries; my guess is that they will all already be on our database, but always worth a look.'

'Thanks for your time and help,' said Jamieson shaking Hess' hand.

Stone stepped forward and shook the big man by the hand: 'Um, gotta ask.' he said, 'Hess?'

Hess nodded. 'Ok. My surname is Moses. In the film the Ten Commandments, Charlton Heston played Moses; Hess is a shortened version of Heston.' He shrugged and grinned apologetically.

Stone nodded. 'It's all about the movies in the gangs unit, isn't it?' He said.

Chapter Ten

Friday 13th November – 10:15

On the drive back to the station, Jamieson's phone rang. He answered whilst driving. It was Peter Jarman, the Chief Constable.

'Alex', he said, 'How goes it?'

'Good morning, Sir.' replied Jamieson. 'Just to give you a heads up, you're on loudspeaker. I'm in the car with DS Stone.' A warning just in case Jarman started down a route that he intended for Jamieson's ears only.

'Sandy,' said Jarman. 'How are you?'

'Good, Sir, thanks for asking.' Said Stone.

'So, Alex, what developments do you have?'

Jamieson had worked for Jarman for a few years now. Jarman lived and died by outcomes - positive ones were expected more often than not. Once in a private conversation, Jarman had admitted to Jamieson that he was more of a politician than a policeman as Chief Constable. He was there as the face of policing. He smiled, delivered promises, and, he hoped, backed those promises up with results.

Results provided by the likes of Jamieson and his team. Jamieson liked this fit. It meant that, for the best part, Jarman left Jamieson to get on with things and relied on Jamieson to report back if he felt intervention from Jarman was required.

Jarman liked the arrangement as well. He surrounded himself with experience as far as he was able. He felt there was no substitute for experience; old hands usually came with cool heads. Usually, Jarman had a question mark around Stone but relied on Jamieson's assurances that 'he was a good policeman' and that was good enough for Jarman.

Jamieson outlined developments so far.

'So, a quick resolution doesn't feel likely?' said Jarman. He liked quick resolutions.

In the car, Jamieson caught Stone's eye and raised his eyebrows. 'Not currently, Sir.' He replied: 'but you know how these cases pan out. Sometimes events gather pace pretty quickly, so let's keep our fingers crossed.'

'Ok, Alex.' said Jarman: 'You don't need to tell me how politically sensitive this one is, a black youth being a victim of knife crime; keep me posted, please.' And as per usual, he was gone without a formal sign-off.

When they returned to the station, Evason's annoyance at missing this morning's meeting seemed to have diminished. Jamieson liked that. He liked that she was initially put out at not being involved in the meeting, and he also liked that she could move on from that annoyance and get on with the nitty-gritty of the case.

Jamieson debriefed them regarding the morning's events and told them he would meet with Jason James this evening.

Johnson picked up. He had researched Macklin Construction and both Macklin Senior and Junior. There was not much to uncover in respect of the business. The local council had awarded some big contracts, but these were won through the usual tender process; nothing to report there; the contracts were carried out satisfactorily. The company balance sheet was strong, and the Directors, Macklin and his wife, were well rewarded. This was borne out by the fact that they lived in a big house in an affluent area.

Personally, Macklin Senior had a relatively clean record, certainly in the last fifteen years or so. Before that, he had a few cautions - fly-tipping and drunk and disorderly - but nothing since.

Michael Macklin, however, was a different matter. Although he had just turned eighteen, he already had a string of offences. More drunk and disorderly, perhaps following in his Father's footsteps, possession of a class B drug, affray on three occasions and - Johnson looked up from his notes - 'Perhaps, most importantly,' he said: 'possession of an offensive weapon, a knife. That was seven months ago.'

'What did he get?' asked Jamieson.

Johnson checked his notes: 'Six months in juvenile detention. He's currently out on licence....' Then, he paused '....and he's tagged. I've put a call into his probation officer. See if we can find out his movements on Wednesday evening.'

'That's interesting. Good work, Rog.' Said, Jamieson.

Evason picked up. She had spoken to the journalist who had written the piece for the local paper. There was not much more to report on that. Confirmation that Ashley was a real talent coveted by some of the biggest and richest football clubs. His Father had taken ownership of Ashley's career and, to avoid what had happened to him, a family decision, which included Ashley, had been made to decline signing for anyone until the boy had reached seventeen. Then it would need to be a minimum of a five-year contract with incremental increases throughout and buyout clauses after the first three years if the right offer came along. The boy was that good.

'One word the journalist used regarding Ashley was 'product'. He said,' she referred to her notes: "It felt like the old man was protecting his product.'

'He also said although Ashley was the topic of the piece that, Jason did most of the talking on his behalf.' She gave a small shrug: 'I guess that's sixteen-year-olds for you. They would rather let someone else do the talking.'

Stone chipped in: 'From speaking with his teacher, I thought there was more to Ashley than that.' He scratched his head. 'Anyway.....'

Johnson's mobile rang. He held it up and looked at Jamieson, who nodded for him to take the call.

Evason continued. Door to door had not thrown up anything else. They had some very grainy footage from CCTV and doorbell cameras but nothing that could be used to identify anyone. There was still no sign of Holly's phone, which was a problem. The ambulance crew team leader was certain she was holding it when they arrived, but now there was no sign of it. They are very busy, but they will thoroughly search the ambulance over the next few days and get back to her.

Finally, Evason concluded: 'I've spoken to the PR team at the Chief Constable's Office, and they have said that it is still a bit early for a press conference, but if no significant progress has been made by, say, Wednesday next week then they will set one up. If she agrees, Holly will need to speak. They will arrange for a blown-up picture of Ashley in the background for the most impact to be made, you know, see if it jogs anyone's memory.'

'Ok, thanks, Claire,' said Jamieson. 'Good stuff.'

Jamieson checked his watch: ten thirty.

He was just about to allocate today's duties when Johnson returned. He looked like the cat that had got the cream.

'Michael Macklin's Probation Officer.' He explained, holding his mobile up.

He took centre stage.

'Michael has been diagnosed with an antisocial personality disorder. This means that he may.....' He referred to his notebook: '........ exploit and manipulate others to his gain, show no remorse for his actions, disregard what is considered normal social behaviour, struggles to maintain relationships, be unable to control his anger, will blame others for problems in his life and will repeatedly break the law.'

'Although it is not known why some people develop this disorder, it is believed that a traumatic childhood experience may bring it on.'

'The current Mrs Macklin is not Michael's birth Mother. Michael's real Mother died when he was seven. She was an alcoholic who took her own life. One day, Michael came home from school and found her hanging in the front room.......'

'Jesus', said Stone: 'Poor little sod.'

Johnson continued: '........It seems Mr Macklin then over-compensated. Threw money at him to do what he wanted with, took him on extravagant holidays, all of that sort of stuff but without really addressing the issue to hand.'

Jamieson nodded: 'Did the Probation Officer think he would be capable of killing Ashley?'

Johnson sighed and puffed out his cheeks: 'If Michael thought that Ashley was responsible for, say, him getting kicked out of the football club, then potentially, yes. It would depend on how Michael perceived the level of, um, treachery. Is that the word?'

Jamieson nodded: 'I think I know what you mean. That would go back to blaming someone else for a situation Michael caused entirely of his own making.'

'One more thing,' said Johnson. 'The GPS tracking map came back for Michael's ankle bracelet for Wednesday evening. At seven thirty, he was on Rankin Avenue about 100 metres from where Ashley James was found with fatal stab wounds.'

Chapter Eleven

Friday 13th November – 14:00

'He was my fucking mate; why would I want to hurt him?' Said, Michael.

Macklin Senior winced at the choice of language.

The clock on the wall showed two o'clock.

The interview room was as full as Jamieson could ever remember.

As well as Michael, there was his father and the family solicitor. Given Michael's age, the Probation Officer had been seconded as an appropriate adult. He'd just turned eighteen, and his complex mental health issues. The job of the appropriate adult was to step in if they felt the individual being questioned was showing signs of stress or the police were acting unfairly. His presence seemed superfluous, but Jamieson wanted to leave nothing to chance.

That was one side of the table.

On the other, there was Jamieson, Evason and Johnson. Johnson was there in an observatory capacity and as a reward for his excellent groundwork so far.

It was stuffy, and someone had body odour. The probation officer looked a fair bet.

Getting all these people in the same room given three hours' notice was a notable achievement. Jamieson suspected that the solicitor jumped whenever Macklin Senior shouted, and the probation officer jumped whenever anyone shouted.

'Tell us about Ashley, Michael?' asked Jamieson.

Michael scratched his chin: 'He was a great footballer. I played in the same team as him at Akley, but I was useless. Ash said, 'don't worry, just have fun, it's all good', and he'd do one of his big smiles; he smiled a lot. But I couldn't hack it in the end. The coaches were always on my back. That bloke, Mcnivett, is it? Twat! So serious. It was all football, no fun. Seriously pissed me off. In the end, I told him to do one and fuck off. So they kicked me out.'

Jamieson nodded: 'Did you stay in touch with Ash?'

Michael considered the question: 'Yeah, but I don't wanna talk about that.' Then, he looked at the solicitor and gestured towards him with his forehead. 'He said I don't have to talk about anything I don't wanna, is that right?'

The solicitor nodded.

'Ok', said Jamieson. This was, without doubt, a reference to the gang to which both boys had membership. Clearly, Michael had some loyalty to Ashley James' memory.

'Now Michael, you have the ankle bracelet on, and you know this means that the probation service can track exactly where you are, yes?' Jamieson held his hands out in front of him in a 'nothing to hide here' gesture.

Michael nodded.

Jamieson continued: 'So we know where you were on Wednesday evening at about half past seven, but I'd like you to tell me in your own words, if you can, please.'

Michael looked at the solicitor, who nodded.

'Look, I know I shouldn't have been, but I was meeting someone on Rankin Avenue around then.' Michael stopped.

'Why was that, Michael?' Prompted Jamieson.

Again, Michael looked towards his solicitor, who again nodded encouragingly.

Michael looked agitated: 'I wanted a bit of blow, not much, just enough to take the edge of things. Sometimes I need to take the edge off things; you know what I mean?'

Before the meeting, Jamieson had assured the solicitor that his team was only interested in the case at hand. They had no interest in minor misdemeanours involving breach of parole or purchasing class B drugs for personal use.

'Who did you see, Michael?' Asked Jamieson.

'Well, I met my man, obviously, and after that, I bumped into Ash.' Macklin Senior stiffened in his chair. The solicitor laid a calming hand on his forearm.

'So', continued Jamieson ', You saw Ash. Did you stop and talk with him? Tell us what happened there.'

'Well, of course, I spoke with him; he's my mate.' Said Michael, confused as to why Jamieson would ask such a question. In his world, you spoke with your mates, didn't you?

'What did you talk about?'

'I asked him where he was going, and he said he was working. He said, 'one more month, Macca,' that's what he called me, 'one more month and I'm out of this.' Then he did one of those big shit-eating grins of his and said 'I'm seventeen soon and the next day I'm signing for......,' well he couldn't say because it was all so secret still. Still, he said it was big, 'I'm going viral, Macca.'

'I was made up for him, really I was, I haven't got many mates, and he was right out there for me if you know what I mean.'

'What else did you talk about, Michael?' asked Jamieson.

'Well, he saw the old tag on my ankle and asked what I'd been up to. So I told him, and he said, 'I'll tell you what, Macca, when I make my debut for my new club, I'll send you some tickets to come and watch, meet some of the other players, have a tour of the ground but,' he said, 'but they don't let your on aeroplanes with a tag on your ankle.....Oops, I've said too much.' Then he gave another grin, hugged me, said he had to go and moved on. That was the last time I saw him.'

'Where did you go after, Michael?' asked Jamieson.

'I turned right up Ranleigh Road and went home on the bus. I was in all evening, you know, smoking........' He shrugged.

'When did you hear about Ash?'

'Someone contacted me on Social Media about ten, I suppose; I was shocked, couldn't believe it, and still can't, if I'm being honest.'

'Michael', said Jamieson ', I have to ask this question, you understand.....' Michael nodded but looked unsure. 'Did you do anything to hurt Ashley James in any way?'

After that, the interview quickly subsided into mayhem. Michael became even more agitated, and the solicitor said he should stop answering further questions. Macklin senior said something about 'hearing from my solicitor' and then realised his solicitor was beside him. The solicitor gave him a withering look that Macklin Senior correctly interpreted as 'shut up'. Ironically, the appropriate adult could find nothing appropriate to say.

Jamieson thanked them for their time and said he might be in touch again in future as the case progressed. However, the solicitor advised that it would have to be under caution next time, not on an informal basis as it had been this time.

Everyone filed out of the room, leaving the musty smell of stale sweat hugging the air.

Chapter Twelve

Friday 13th November – 18:15

Jamieson checked his watch: six fifteen.

He was driving home, and the rain continued to thrash down. Progress was slow. Drivers were overcompensating for the conditions. He was at least fifty minutes from home, and then he needed to change and get down to Akley Football Club. He would miss kick-off, almost certainly.

Before he had left the office, they had had a debrief of the day.

The team had done some solid work, and progress had been made. Michael Macklin was a person of interest, for sure. However, some of his responses, particularly those concerning Ashley, seemed to be so heartfelt, so honest, that a big part of Jamieson struggled to believe anything other than the answers that Michael Macklin had given.

He had asked Stone and Evason to arrange a visit to Holly Matthews on Saturday morning. Given the passing of time, she may be able to talk with more clarity. Perhaps the shock had subsided. Hopefully, she would be more coherent in the mornings with her judgement not clouded by what-ever she was taking.

As he left, as was customary, he thanked them for their efforts to date. He enjoyed working with this team. Ok, some of the work they had to deal with was distasteful and distressing, but they all did it with professionalism and, for the best part, good humour.

Halfway down the corridor, he remembered some-thing and spun on his heel. He poked his head back around the door.

'Thought you'd gone', said Stone.

Jamieson ignored him: 'While I remember,' he said, 'put 11th December in your diaries, call it a Christmas party; I've bought you all two tickets for a charity event at the Bell pub near where I live. Live music and a buffet, I'll even stand a round of drinks. So bring someone you love, and that doesn't mean you can come twice, Sandy.'

'This live music,' asked Stone. 'Is it the Wailing Bun-nies?'

A smile played on Jamieson's lips; he'd been sussed: 'It is indeed the Wailing Bunnies.' And before anyone could ask any more questions, he was gone.

'The Wailing Bunnies?' said Johnson, with an amused look.

Stone sat back in his chair, fingers of each hand locked together behind his head. Even Evason was perplexed with this one.

'Yes, that is the name of the boss's band.' Confirmed Stone.

'His band?' said Evason. 'What do you mean his band?'

'I mean', said Stone ', the band in which he occasionally plays guitar and would undoubtedly do so more often if he wasn't here solving crimes.'

'And I have to say,' He continued, 'that I may be an old man with questionable tastes in music, but I, for one, think they are bloody good. So it will be a good evening and deserving of our support.'

'Well,' said Evason, 'That is something I did not expect to learn today.' Genuine surprise strung across her face, 'and I, for one, will certainly be there.'

Johnson slowly shook his head, still taking it in: 'Me too,' he said, 'not sure that is something I'd want to miss.'

'I'll tell you one last thing.' Stone said. 'His moment of glory comes in a song called 'Johnny B. Goode'. So, go home, download the Chuck Berry version, play it, memorise it, and when your boss moves centre stage, we'll all be there singing along with him. Of course, it will embarrass the hell out of him, but he will absolutely love it!'

Chapter Thirteen

Friday 13th November – 19:45

Jamieson pushed through the old turnstile, having paid his ten-pound entry fee.

He was handed a printed sheet showing the names of those playing and the referees. The match was a fourth-round District League cup match versus local rivals Leighbridge.

At the bottom of the sheet, the words 'In memory of Ashley James' had been typed.

The rain had eased off, but it still came down. He was slightly late and had missed the kick-off by ten minutes.

The ground had a floodlight in each corner, but they were not overly effective. The poor weather and darkness at this time of the year made it difficult to pick out the players. However, Jamieson acknowledged that he hadn't been to the opticians in a while.

The ground had a loosely termed main stand with seating, and that was where he headed. Entry was from the back of the stand, and he stood at the top of the stairs scanning the heads for someone he thought was Jason James. There were probably only twenty or so brave souls who had ventured out.

At the front, he saw Davey Mcniven sitting behind where the team dugout was. It seemed Mcniven acted in some capacity in every aspect of this club. Now he had a bag with him, and it appeared that he was doing the role of trainer in case anyone got injured. Jamieson went down the stairs towards him.

'Mr Mcniven.' He said. 'Good evening.'

Mcniven jumped. He was clearly of a nervous disposition. 'Oh, hello.' He said. He had forgotten Jamieson's name, and for a brief moment, his mouth moved without any words coming out. He finally decided it was better to say nothing else.

'I was looking for Jason James. He said he'd be here this evening.'

'Yes. He is,' said Mcniven. He pointed to a solitary figure standing behind one of the goals leaning on the crash barrier. He could see Jamieson's astonishment as to why anyone would want to stand out in the rain when there was cover in the main stand. He apologetically smiled and shrugged: 'It's where he always stands when he comes here.' He said by way of an explanation.

'Thanks', said Jamieson and turned to go, but he stopped and turned back. 'Any score?' He asked.

Mcniven raised his eyebrows: 'The opposition is one up. Good strike, but our keeper should probably have kept it out.' He looked at his watch. 'Long time to go still.'

'Fingers crossed', said Jamieson and made his way back up the main stand to get to where James was.

Jamieson was well-kitted out for the weather. He wore a waxed jacket, jeans and his walking boots. In addition, he'd found an old flat cap that belonged to his eldest, Xander but just about fitted. As he approached, James straightened himself up and offered his hand. 'Alex', he said. Jamieson shook it. 'Jason', he said. Jayce or JJ still felt a bit overly friendly.

James resumed leaning against the crash barrier, and Jamieson felt obliged to copy him. Together they watched the play for a couple of minutes.

Finally, Jamieson asked: 'How are things?' Pretty stupid question given the circumstances; however, he couldn't think of anything that might be more appropriate.

'Ah, you know. Shit, but there you have it. What are you going to do about it?' A rhetorical question. 'They held a minute's applause for Ash. You know, before kick-off, which was nice. Quite pleased you missed it because I was bawling my eyes out.'

'The Chairman called yesterday and asked if I thought the game should be called off. The opposition had heard about what had happened and offered to rearrange. I thought it was a lovely gesture but that it should go ahead. The kid lived for football, so why would he want it to be cancelled? The Chairman said the club would do a proper tribute at the next first-team game. You know, Ash's photo on the front cover of the programme and a write-up about him inside. I'm grateful. They're good people, and this club has been a massive part of Ash's life - mine too.'

'Have you seen Holly?' asked Jamieson.

'Yes. She was wasted. I'm not sure if it was booze or drugs. I couldn't get much out of her; she just cried and sobbed the whole time. I spoke to 'the gatekeeper', that's what I call her Mother, a horrible woman. We decided on a family funeral with no flowers and any donations to victims of knife crime, seemed appropriate, really. Your lot have released Ash to the funeral home. It's just a case of getting a date in the diary that works for everyone. Depending on when that is, I may go back to Spain and come back again. I've got commitments out there to deal with. All the other things don't just stop even though it feels they should.'

Jamieson noticed that play on the pitch had stopped for an injury. Mcniven was crouched over a prone player applying spray to his ankle. He seemed to know what he was doing.

'How did Spain come about?' He asked.

'Opportunity,' said James: 'I'm sure that Davey told you about my experience with professional football. How I was signed at eleven and unceremoniously dumped just before I was sixteen. So there I was, no future, no qualifications, I played at a reasonable level for a while, but I had to work as a delivery driver to get some money coming in. When I was about twenty, I met Holly, she was probably seventeen then. She was beautiful. She loved me. I was still a bit bruised over not being a professional footballer, and she was just bruised full stop. She was very delicate in those days, very vulnerable. Her problems had always been there, but when we were together, it was like they disappeared.'

'Anyway, I got a call from an old mate living in Spain. He said the local team were looking for players, and he thought of me. They played four divisions down from La

Liga, where the big sides played, and the deal was a good one, so I went out there for a week to look.'

James fell silent as he watched the game. Then, suddenly animated, he bawled 'Ref' when the official failed to award a free kick to Akley.

'When I got out to Spain, there was a reason they were looking at players like me. Spanish football had an awful reputation for racism, and they wanted to do something about it. So there was a positive drive to recruit black players into the lower leagues.'

'I wasn't sure how I felt about it a first. When one of my good friends said, 'so you'll be the token black,' whilst I don't think he meant anything by it, it felt a bit like that. Kind of; we only really want you because of your skin colour. My old man was still alive back then, so I spoke to him about it, and he said, 'look, son, if you weren't there as the token black, there would be no black players playing at all, and that would be a crime. You're a good footballer, go over there and give them your best. It's the only way that attitudes towards race will ever change.'

'So, I phoned Holly and said, 'come on, let's do it; let's move away from all the negativity at home and make a brand-new start out here'. She went very quiet and said, 'Jayce, I'm pregnant.'

'I was over the moon. I was going to be a dad. 'Fantastic.' I said: 'You can have the baby in the UK, and then we can move out here. That was the plan anyway.' He gave a rueful smile.

'So, I went to Spain and flew back every few weeks. She had a great pregnancy and really flourished, but every time I went back, I could feel that her Mother was getting her claws further and further into Holly. Ironic, really, because when Hol was growing up, her Mother had very little interest in her. Now she looked like she was getting a bit of happiness in her life; there was her Mother to stamp all over it. Anyway, Ash was born, but every time I suggested making plans about the move, Hol was, 'not just yet, I need Mum around to help me,' and all the time, the old toad sat in the corner with a self-satisfied smile on her face, it was almost like she was saying 'she ain't coming, I'm gonna fuck up your plans.'

Just then, the half-time whistle sounded, and the players trooped off through the rain: 'Come on,' said James, 'I'll buy you that Bovril.'

They returned to the bar area, which served hot drinks and snacks at half-time, then alcoholic drinks after the game. Jamieson opted for tea. Clearly, James was well thought of at the club. People were approaching him, offering handshakes and sympathetic pats on the back. Few knew what to say, but a look and a sad smile were enough. One older lady with tears in her eyes hugged him and tried to say something, but in the end, gave up, patted his arm and moved away to where her husband was sitting, and her hot drink awaited.

They made small talk, the players and officials reappeared on the pitch, and the game restarted. The rain continued. Jamieson and James made their way back to where they had stood previously.

James picked up again: 'So for a couple of years, I travelled back and forth between Spain and the UK. The football was fine. There were a few problems initially, but I think more and more black players started appearing in the higher leagues and certainly for the bigger clubs, so the attitude softened. There was the odd occasion that a big defender would boot me up in the air and mutter 'bastardo negro'. No prizes for that translation, but overall, it was good. Then Holly fell pregnant again. Not so good this time. I was still going back every three weeks, but I felt something was different. I thought about jacking the whole Spain thing in, but the money was good, and I honestly still thought that we would eventually get out there despite what her Mother might think.'

'Then, when the baby was born, the proverbial really hit the fan. He was white with blond hair; it couldn't have been mine, impossible. Then one of my mates told me Holly was back to her old ways. She'd leave Ash with her mum and meet up with all the winos and druggies she used to hang around with. I know she was vulnerable and couldn't help herself, but I couldn't deal with it. I walked away from her. I often think back and wonder whether I should have supported her better. I mean, I still came home on the same basis and provided money for Ash and a bit extra for the new baby. It wasn't the poor kid's fault, the circumstances he'd been born into. I wondered how much money I sent back was used to keep Holly on drugs.'

The referee gave a red card to one of the Akley players, and he almost looked grateful to be given the opportunity to first use the showers as he trudged off.

James looked dejected; 'I was so proud of Ash. Despite everything he had to endure, he had grown up to be such a well-adjusted kid. He excelled at everything he put his mind to. He was popular; he was kind. I can't believe it's all gone.'

Jamieson found himself in the same position as the people at half-time - he had no idea what to say.

'Have you got any idea what he was doing there at that time? I mean, it's a couple of miles from home. I know that Holly found him, but I couldn't get any sense out of her. What was he doing there? What was she doing there? Was it drugs? I just don't know.' James sounded desperate.

'In honesty,' said Jamieson ', we don't know too much at present. There's always rumours when something like this happens.'

'What sort of rumours?' asked James.

Jamieson shrugged: 'Getting in with the wrong crowd. That sort of thing, something and nothing is all.'

'Someone at the club? Who? Not that Macklin kid?' Demanded James.

Jamieson knew he had already said too much. 'No. My sergeant had picked up on it, but no names were mentioned. We'll need to look into it as the investigation moves on.'

A silence fell between the two men. Akley conceded two quick goals on the pitch to effectively end the match as a contest. Jamieson saw his opportunity to slip away.

He offered his hand to James: 'I'm going to make a move.' He said. 'It was good to spend some time with you, and once again, I am so sorry about Ash.'

James took the offered hand: 'Alex,' he said, 'Thanks for your time and for listening to my woes.' He smiled. 'Under normal circumstances, I can be fun to be with, I promise you. If you need anything, give me a call. You've got my number.'

Jamieson set off back towards the exit behind the main stand. On the way, Akley conceded again. Perhaps they should have accepted the oppo's offer and called this one off.

Chapter Fourteen

Saturday 14th November – 09:15

Welwyn Garden City is a town in Hertfordshire, England, some 20 miles north of London. It was the second garden city in England behind Letchworth. It was designated one of the first new towns in 1948 as Britain sought to recover from the second world war.

Welwyn Garden City was founded by Sir Ebenezer Howard in 1920, who had called for the creation of planned towns to combine the benefits of the city and the countryside and to avoid the disadvantages of both.

His design was thought to represent 'The Perfect Town'. No one ever questioned why a 'city' was considered a perfect 'town'.

On this particular day, Welwyn was living up to its title of 'garden city'. The past few days' rain gave it a green and vibrant feel. However, there were still trees where leaves had turned from green to a golden brown ready to drop as winter approached.

Many of the streets were tree-lined, and the overall ambience was one of fresh, new beginnings.

Sir Ebenezer would have been very pleased.

Roy Mcniven sat at the breakfast bar in the kitchen of his three-bed semi. He had a cup of tea, and a slice of toast with marmalade smeared liberally across the surface.

Roy was a traditionalist at heart, marmalade, always marmalade on toast for breakfast.

He took a bite from the toast and turned the page of the newspaper, delivered daily, which sat on the bar in front of him. When he read a newspaper, he always read the first five pages from the front and then flipped it over to read the sports pages from the back inwards. Then the television listings. Then a final complete read-through to cover everything that he had missed.

Then he turned to the crossword puzzle, cryptic but not too cryptic. Roy usually finished it in fifteen minutes.

Today he was struggling because there was something on his mind. So he rubbed his hand across his chin and refocused his efforts on the crossword.

He filled in two answers before the door opened.

His wife, Maureen, came into the kitchen and sighed.

'That bad, eh?' asked Roy.

Maureen widened her eyes. 'I don't know, Roy. What if he's broken the law? What if he's in real trouble? I'm not sure what we're doing is the best thing.'

Roy drew breath and released it slowly through his nostrils. 'I know, love, but he's our son, right? You know what they say about blood being thicker than water. I wish I knew what was going on, but we have to trust him, don't we? He said it was for a few days, and we can do that for him, can't we? Trust him, I mean.' He shrugged.

Maureen wrung a tea towel through her hands. Suddenly her face crumpled, and she dissolved into tears. 'Oh, Roy.' She said.

Roy was up off her seat and wrapping his arms around her: 'Come on, love. It's just a couple of days. We can do that for him, can't we?'

Maureen sniffed. Through her tears, she said: 'I suppose so.'

Chapter Fifteen

Saturday 14th November – 09:30

Stone picked Evason up from home at nine-thirty. No need to be going into the office, not just yet anyway.

Evason had phoned yesterday and told Mrs Matthews they would call at ten o'clock to find out if Holly had remembered anything more. In her usual brusque manner, the older Matthews woman told them: 'Good luck with that, Hol don't usually surface until mid-day most days.'

In her most professional manner, Evason replied: 'We'd be grateful if you could make sure that she's ready for us so we can find out who killed her son that much quicker.'

Evason also learned more about the payments made to reduce the rent arrears. The council had issued an old-style payment book where their tenants could pay cash directly in at a bank, and the payment would find its way into the tenant's rent account with the council. In the past nine months, payments of twelve thousand pounds had been made in cash.

Evason also did some digging around the other amenities. Electricity, gas, water and council tax were all up to date, with payments made similarly. By cash at a bank.

Someone was getting their hands on an awful lot of cash.

Stone parked up just past the address that they had for Holly Matthews.

For social housing, the area was in good order. There was a green and a playground for kids to play, but not today; the rain continued to hammer down. The houses themselves looked to be recently built, their newness adding to the overall good look and feel of the area.

Stone looked across at Evason: 'You lead,' he said, 'I think I might get annoyed quite quickly by Mum.'

Evason smiled: 'Yes, I can see that being the case.' She said.

They made the mad dash from the car to the front door in a brief respite from the rain and huddled together under the small porch. The close proximity was awkward. Although Stone and Evason worked well in a team, they rarely doubled up in the field, as it were. This was down to good management by Jamieson. Jamieson knew that although there was mutual respect from both parties, on occasion, Evason considered Stone a bit of a dinosaur, and Stone thought Evason to be a 'bit bloody high and mighty', his words. As a result, Jamieson kept them apart insofar as he was able. Today was an exception, and Jamieson thought that on this occasion, they would have to 'behave and play nicely'.

Evason rang the doorbell, which gave a resounding 'bing-bong' inside the house.

After a few more uncomfortable minutes - was Stone breathing through his mouth on purpose, thought Evason - the huge figure of Mrs Matthews lurched into sight down the hallway. The door finally opened, and the big woman just turned and walked back down the hallway without a word. Evason and Stone took this as an invitation to follow and close the door behind them.

'She's still half stoned from last night.' Mrs Matthews announced over her shoulder before turning into what turned out to be the living room.

The two girls were quietly doing a jigsaw puzzle on the big table. Holly was propped up on the sofa, wearing her dressing gown and staring at the television, some cookery programme, with the sound, turned down. She didn't look up when they entered but muttered something under her breath which sounded very much like 'bit fuckin' early for this.'

Mrs Matthews maneuvered above the vacant space on the sofa before dropping herself in with an 'oooffff'. The sofa creaked but held firm.

Evason pulled a chair from the table, sat, and took out her notebook. Stone remained standing in the doorway.

Evason deliberately kept her voice to almost a whisper: 'How are the girls doing?' She directed her question towards Holly.

Mrs Matthews answered: 'They know, but they're too young to understand, really. The little one keeps asking when Ash is coming home. The older one gets it a bit better, but still, it's hard on them. It's hard on us all.'

'What about Lewis? How has he taken it?' Asked Evason.

Again, Mrs Matthews answered: 'He's still with his father's family. They've told him, and he's pretty cut up, as you'd expect. It's better he stays with them for the time being. They can take his mind off things better than we can here. Everywhere you look here, there's memories to be had.'

'How long has he been with them?' Asked Evason.

'Eeerrrm,' the big woman shrugged, 'beginning of the week. I think he was dropped off on Monday evening.

Evason realised that she would have to address Holly directly to prevent the older woman from answering.

'Holly', she said, 'Have you remembered anything else about Wednesday evening since we last spoke?'

Holly lifted her head and looked at Evason through blurry eyes. She shook her head slowly.

Evason flicked through her notebook. 'I'm just going to go over what you told us again. See if it jogs anything in your memory, if that's okay with you?'

This time Holly nodded. Evason went through everything that Holly had told her and Jamieson in the hospital on Thursday morning. Holly appeared to be listening intently but could find nothing to add.

The situation reached an impasse. Evason started to put her notebook away and gather her belongings, readying herself to leave.

Mrs Matthews spoke: 'Tell 'em what you told me, Hol.' The girl looked at her blankly. 'You know, about who you saw.' She prompted.

Holly leant forward and put her elbows on her knees, staring at the floor in front of her, trying to remember what the older woman was referring to.

Suddenly she lifted her head: 'Yeah, right' she said 'I did see someone else that night. One of the boys who played football with my Ash. I think they called him Mac or something like that.' She screwed up her eyes, trying to remember exactly.

'Macca?' said Evason. 'Michael Macklin?'

'Think so.', said Holly. 'Big lad. Ash liked him.'

'Well, not really.' Interjected Mrs Matthews. 'He was trouble from the very start.'

'Where was this, Holly?' asked Evason, but she could see that the girl had already returned her gaze to the television set where a minor celebrity was enjoining a plate of something that a minor celebrity chef had prepared.

That was the end of that. They stayed for another ten minutes, but Holly had switched off and, by the time they took their leave, had dozed off on the sofa.

They stood to leave, and the ever gracious Mrs Matthews had the final word: 'You can show yourselves out,' she muttered.

Back in the car, Evason asked Stone what he made of it.

'Well,' replied Stone ', Michael Macklin's name has come up again, but in fairness to him, he had already told us that he had seen Ashley, so nothing new to go on there.'

'Mmmm', said Evason, in a noncommittal way, 'We need to speak to a sober Holly without the spectre of Mrs Matthews policing everything that she says. Did the mention of Macklin feel a bit staged to you?'

'Maybe', said Stone. 'It certainly didn't flow, did it?'

Just then, Stone's phone rang. He didn't recognise the number on the dashboard display but answered it anyway.

'Stone', he said.

'Oh', said a female voice. 'Is that Detective Sergeant Stone?'

'Speaking'

'It's Helen Miller from the school. We met the other day.'

'Ah yes, Mrs Miller. What can I do for you?'

'Well, I just wanted to thank you again for what you did for the children and staff. It was a very courageous thing to do, to stand up in front of a crowd of people that you didn't know and talk the way you did and say the things you said.'

In the passenger seat, Evason listened intently with a quizzical look on her face. Stone realised that the only person in the team aware of these events was Johnson, and Stone had sworn him to secrecy.

'Please don't mention it; it really was the least I could do.' Said Stone, hoping he'd closed that line of conversation down before Evason heard too much.

'No, it really was fantastic and has helped the process hugely,' continued Helen.

'No problem.' said a flustered Stone.

'I wondered,' said Helen. 'I couldn't help but notice that you weren't wearing a wedding ring, and, erm...., well, would you like to go out for a drink sometime?'

Evason's face positively broke into a huge grin. She was enjoying this very much indeed.

This time Stone stalled over his words: 'I'm sorry I should have made it clear that I'm not alone in the car; one of my colleagues...........'

'Oh God!' said Helen, and the line went dead.

Stone went puce. Sitting next to him, Evason was trying to unsuccessfully suppress her laughter. Tears were rolling down her cheeks.

Eventually, Stone could not help but join in and had to pull over for fear of causing an accident.

'I do believe,' said Evason between fits of laughter, 'that you've just been chatted up in front of a live audience.'

'Oh Jesus', said Stone through his own tears ', I suppose I should take it as a compliment.'

They sat and giggled for a further five minutes.

Team building? Jamieson would have loved it.

Chapter Sixteen

Saturday 14th November – 15:10

Liz Matthews was a vengeful person.

She stood outside in the rain watching over her two young granddaughters. It continued to hammer down, but they had all been in a crowded apartment for the past three days, and it was frankly driving her mad.

The girls were well wrapped up against the elements. They wore pink coats and wellington boots as they ran around the playground, splashing in puddles and generally shouting and screaming. Letting off steam, Liz's Mother would have said.

Liz was standing under some trees which offered shelter from the onslaught of the driving rain but which now and again delivered a big drop onto the hood of her anorak.

She was trying to smoke without the girls seeing her. They would tell Holly, and one seemingly small act would get blown out of all proportion like it normally did. Then Liz and her daughter would sit in silence all evening, simmering to the point of overboiling.

For the last thirty years or so, Liz had been angry.

Anger was her overriding emotion – anger at everything. Even now, and the tragedy that the family found themselves faced with, Liz Matthews found it difficult, no impossible, to grieve for her grandson. Instead, it was anger that consumed her.

She hadn't always been this way. When Holly was born thirty-five years ago, she was relatively happy.

Holly had a father, and she had a husband. And while he wouldn't hesitate to slap Liz to keep her in line, he was a decent enough provider. The flat of his hand Liz could cope with; the balled fist was always another matter. When she was out with her friends, which was seldom, they all had similar stories. They were the days of putting up and shutting up.

His name was John McClelland, and he stood well over six feet tall. His imaginative friends called him Big Mac. He worked down on the docks, and he worked hard long hours. He would leave the house around six thirty each weekday morning and would not return until seven, except for Fridays. Fridays were when Big Mac and his friends unwound and relaxed. Those evenings he wouldn't return until after closing time and would stink of beer and fags. She would have to submit to him and his lust during those times. It was not pleasurable for her. It hurt a great deal. However, she consoled herself that it didn't last long, and he would soon roll off her and fall asleep, snoring and grunting.

She would take herself off to the bathroom where she would douche herself thoroughly – she didn't want another child, and Big Mac didn't believe in using condoms – she would have a little cry to herself and then creep into Holly's bed where Mother and daughter would snuggle up together and sleep through until morning.

When Holly was eight, Big Mac was out on one of his Friday nights and on his way home, severely drunk, he tried to cross a dual carriageway. He got halfway across when he was clipped by a MacDonald's lorry – ironic given his nickname – which spun him into the path of a speeding car. The driver slammed the brakes on but still smashed into Big Mac. The impact threw him forty metres away. According to the doctors, he landed on his head and was probably brain-dead before his limp body settled to a halt. He was put on a life support machine primarily so his organs could be used for transplant – well, his liver was screwed from the booze, and his lungs shot from his excessive smoking – but they had the rest. Liz never found out if they were used or not.

A few weeks later, when Liz was clearing through some of Big Mac's old paperwork, she discovered he had cancelled a life insurance policy which would have paid out over a hundred thousand pounds two weeks before the accident. The premium was two pounds seventy-five a month. He had just written across the lapsed policy in red ink - 'too fucking expensive'. Back then, two pounds seventy-five would have paid for the price of two pints of beer.

Big Mac's employers paid her their death in service package, which equated to six months' salary. That would be around nine thousand pounds. The cheque was for three and a half thousand pounds when she received it. Big Mac, it seemed, had been drawing against his future salary to pay for his booze and a nasty little gambling habit that he had picked up.

This was when Liz Matthews got angry.

She got angry with the local housing office when they told her she no longer qualified for a two-bedroomed council property and tried to move her into a studio flat.

She got angry with the benefits' office when they told her that Big Mac was behind with his National Insurance contributions and that she wouldn't qualify for the full benefit she would have been entitled to under normal circumstances.

She got angry with the schools when they told her that Holly's learning and emotional levels were inconsistent with a girl her age.

But she got most angry when Holly said she was glad her dad was dead because he couldn't get into bed with her anymore; she didn't like that.

Liz simmered.

They were better off without the nasty bastard, but he hadn't left them in a good place.

Liz coerced her Mother to move in with them; at least during the week, her father would have to learn to care for himself from Monday through Friday. It's not as if he wasn't capable; he was just lazy.

Liz then set about finding work to provide an income. Unfortunately, she would need two jobs because she had no qualifications to find a single job that attracted a reasonable wage. Despite all of her shortcomings, she was a conscientious worker. If someone was paying her money, she felt it was fair and proper that they received value for their investment.

She took a day job with a supermarket, stacking shelves, and an evening job cleaning local offices. Both jobs were Monday to Friday. She needed to be on shift at the supermarket at seven forty-five in the morning and finished at five. She then spent an hour at home with Holly and grabbed some dinner before cleaning offices at six thirty for as long as it took. This was usually until nine. Some of these office workers were disgusting, and the toilets were a disgrace, but she did what she had to.

Weekends were for her and Holly. There were two reasons for this.

Firstly, she recognised that she could not sustain the level of work that she was doing without getting a reasonable break; for her, it was physically impossible; she would break.

Secondly, it had slowly dawned on Liz that Holly was damaged. Despite her anger at the school, they were right. Emotionally and educationally, the girl was stunted. Coupled with the abuse her father was subjecting her to, it was no surprise Holly was withdrawn. She rarely laughed or smiled and seldom mentioned friends. Liz wasn't sure whether she had any.

So weekends were their time together, and, at first, it worked. Holly came out of her shell and started engaging more at school. She made friends and even attended sleepovers. Her schoolwork improved beyond recognition. Liz always felt she was a bright girl; now her grades and predictions confirm that.

The next four years were as good as it got for the family. They even managed a couple of holidays at a caravan park on the south coast with Liz's parents, which still provided Liz with some of her fondest memories.

But in anyone's book, four years is a long time.

As Holly neared her teenage years and all the baggage that bought for a young woman, Liz's parents lurched towards their twilight years, laced with their own uncertainties.

At seventy-three, Liz's Dad was diagnosed with early-onset dementia, quickly progressing to full-blown dementia. All of her Mother's time was taken up caring for him, and the arrangement to look after Holly for the weekdays when Liz wasn't able to through work commitments fell away. In theory, Holly was old enough to look after herself, but her history worried Liz. Financially Liz could not afford to drop either job, so Holly had to become self-sufficient and care for herself at thirteen.

Without the structure of her home life, Holly wouldn't take long to veer from the rails. At first, Liz closed her eyes to the situation and blamed Holly's age on the worrying reports coming from the school.

Liz shielded her cigarette in her cupped hand behind her back as she called to the girls: 'Five more minutes, I'm starting to get wet here.'

They either didn't hear or chose to ignore her as they continued to burn off the excess energy from the past few days.

Liz watched as two young girls, bundled up against the weather, went up the garden path and knocked on the door of their home. They had a bunch of flowers with them.

Liz didn't move, she'd let Holly deal with this, but she continued watching. Finally, after a couple of minutes, the door opened, and Holly appeared; she chatted with the girls for a minute and took the flowers. Then she closed the door, and the girls left the way they had arrived.

Liz took a final drag on her cigarette, threw the butt down and crushed it under her foot.

She could not stop herself from thinking that for the second time in her life, her insurance policy because that was what Ashley was, had been cancelled before she had the opportunity of it paying out.

And that made her even angrier.

Chapter Seventeen

Saturday 14th November - 15:15

Holly wrapped her arms tighter around herself.

She looked out of the window. She knew that her mother and the girls were out there, she could hear the girls screaming, but right now, she concentrated solely on the rain as it hammered into the glass. She would pick out individual raindrops and watch them as they slid down the window.

She examined her fingers. There was still blood around the edges of her nails.

Ashley's blood.

She could not bring herself to wash her hands. That would mean washing away her son's last vestiges, the boy's last physical traces.

'Train wreck' Holly. That had been a cruel nickname bestowed upon her at school. At thirteen, she had quickly slid from a promising student to a no-hoper, one for the scrap heap.

She knew that she had picked up with the wrong crowd. She just couldn't resist the lure. The glamour that went with being one of the cool kids. She had lost her support network – Nan was at home looking after Grandad, and her mother was too busy working – it was no wonder that Holly was going off track. There was no one around to police her. She couldn't do it herself; for God's sake, she was only just a teenager.

She gave herself cheaply to the boys. The first time she was fourteen (Daddy didn't count). She was at least at home in her own bed at the time – mum was on an evening shift cleaning offices – Holly thought the boy liked her, but it had hurt, and she had bled badly. Afterwards, she cried, and the boy, who was seventeen, gave her a pill. He told her it would take away the pain and make her feel good.

And it did for an hour at least.

After that, they met once a week for a repeat performance. It wasn't the physical act of sex that she enjoyed; she hated it, but she would put up with that for the magic pill the boy gave her each week. The pill, that for one hour, took her away from the pain of her life.

She then found herself sinking into periods of darkness and despair. Finally, she told her mother, who cruelly told her that was life, and she needed to get on with it. She was fifteen at the time.

Finally, she took herself to the doctor, who referred her to a mental health team. She was diagnosed as bipolar with obsessive-compulsive traits and given medication. But, unfortunately, her mother's attitude did not soften; if anything, it went the other way.

After two years of drifting along with the wrong crowd, she met Jason James.

A friend had taken her to watch Akley FC. The friend was meeting a dealer. Holly enjoyed the football, and that surprised her. What surprised her was that one of the players caught her eye, a slightly built, black kid playing for Akley. He had the number nine on the back of his shirt.

After the match had finished, they went to the club bar, and number nine came in after showering. He smiled at her as he walked past on his way to the bar.

She went back the next week, and he smiled at her again.

It became a weekly occurrence. It became a high point in Holly's week. The build-up to an evening at Akley FC and an encounter with number nine, however brief.

Finally, after the fifth or sixth week, he spoke to her. Something like 'we've been seeing a lot of you at Akley recently', but she felt special, perhaps for the first time in her life.

The following week he sat with her, and she found out more about him. His name was Jason James, and he was twenty-one. He asked her what she did at the weekend, and when she said, 'not much', he asked her out.

They saw more and more of each other over the next few months. Holly was as besotted with Jason as he was with her. He got her, understood her, knew about her pain, and just his presence put it right. Suddenly Jason was needed; he felt needed. This damaged young woman needed him, and he loved her for it.

Two weeks after her eighteenth birthday Holly fell pregnant.

They were both surprised but very happy, although this meant the introduction of an, as yet, unaware third party – Holly's Mother, Liz.

To date, Liz didn't know about Jason. However, she knew her daughter was seeing someone; her whole demeanour had changed. She was back to the bright and breezy thirteen-year-old. In short, she was happy.

Holly was worried. Not so much that Jason was black and Liz was racist. With Liz, it went deeper than that. She disliked everyone regardless of race, sex, religion, or sexual preference. Holly looked up the word for this – misanthropy – a general hatred, dislike, distrust or contempt of the human species, human behaviour or human nature. That about summed Liz up.

They decided on the sticking plaster approach – do it quickly, and it won't hurt so much for so long. So after her 12-week scan showed that everything was going according to plan, and before Holly started to show or have anything like morning sickness, Holly took Jason home one evening. When Liz got in from her evening cleaning shift, Holly asked her to sit down.

'This,' she announced, 'is Jason.' Jason appeared. Holly continued: 'We've been together for nearly six months now, and..,' she stalled, her confidence drying up, '...and, we going to have a baby together. He will be moving in with us so we can bring the baby up as a family.'

Holly stepped back and waited for an explosion.

It never came.

Liz sniffed and said: 'Whatever.' And went to bed.

Jason moved in, and an uneasy truce fell across the home.

Holly grew bigger and flourished during pregnancy. Then, just before Christmas 2002, she gave birth to Ashley. A healthy, beautiful baby. Even Liz said so.

For a year, Holly was as happy as she had ever been. She loved Ashley with all her heart. Jason was a loving father; even her mother had softened a little. Holly continued to take her medication; she knew it was all part of her own personal jigsaw. Everything needed to be in place to make it work well.

The only slight cloud was with Jason. She knew he felt unfulfilled. He was doing a delivery job during the day and turning out for Akley FC for mid-week games and on Saturdays. There was a small payment for playing for the team, but still, even with what he made from the delivery job, things were very tight. Holidays and treats were out of the question. They just could not afford them.

So it was no surprise when Jason came home after a Saturday match almost fit to burst. Someone down the club had a contact in Spain, and they were looking for players. And Jason fit the bill exactly.

The job came with accommodation and a good salary, far more than he was currently earning, and the cost of living was cheaper in Spain, so they could live like kings.

'Think, Hol,' he said. 'What an opportunity! What a place to bring a family up in! Great weather all year round. Our own place.' God, he was so excited she thought he might just explode!

And she wanted to go; she really did.

But there was her mother. What about poor, old Liz?

They went out to Spain for a few days, the first time Holly had ever been abroad, and, she had to admit, it was like a dream.

But what about poor, old Liz?

In the end, Jason took the contract up with the proviso that he could come home every three weeks or so, matches permitting. Holly would join him when she felt more confident with Ashley and was no longer reliant on her mother for support. That was what her mother had suggested anyway, and Holly had agreed. After all, as her mother had told her, there was no way she could cope with Ashley on her own, not without her mother's support.

At first, it worked well. Jason sent money home, and, as promised, he came home every three to four weeks to spend time with her and Ashley. He seemed so happy, and that made *her* happy.

However, she missed Jason.

She missed him so much that it physically hurt. She could feel herself slipping back into her old ways. She started seeing her old friends again, her bad friends, and soon her old addictions resurfaced. And, as she reflected, the most horrible thing was that her mother could see what was happening and did nothing about it. She just let it happen, her own daughter; she just let her slip back into her old ways.

Then Holly fell pregnant again. She panicked. She hoped it was Jason's, but deep down, she knew it could be any one of at least three other men. That wasn't good odds.

This pregnancy was the polar opposite of her last one. She missed Jason. She had awful morning sickness. Her back ached all the time, and, worse of all, she still hung out with her 'friends'. But, she couldn't help it.

She was in labour for over twenty hours. At least that gave Jason time to book a flight and get home before the baby was born. That was the plan anyway.

But it went to shit. The baby was white. Jason walked out of the delivery room. She was alone again.

Her thoughts were interrupted by the doorbell. She then realised it was probably the second or third time it had been rung. She had heard it each time; it just hadn't registered.

She went down the hall and opened the door. Two girls, wrapped up against the rain, stood there. Holly could tell that they had been crying. One of the girls pushed a bunch of flowers towards her: 'We're so sorry about Ashley.' She said: 'We all loved him at school. We can't believe it.' She stood shaking her head.

Holly could have swept them into her arms and comforted them, but she didn't know how to. No one had done that to her, so she didn't know what to do. It was all so unnatural to her.

Instead, she gave a sad smile: 'Thank you' was all she could think of to say.

She closed the door. She went to the kitchen and put the bouquet down amongst the other twenty or so that had already been received.

Then the tears came again. Everyone so loved Ashley. How on God's earth had this happened?

Outside, she heard the girls scream and laugh as they played in the pouring rain.

Chapter Eighteen

Saturday 14th November – 15:20

Jason James stood in exactly the same spot as the previous evening alongside Alex Jamieson.

The rain continued to thrash down, but James hardly noticed. A match was being played in front of him, but again it barely registered.

For Jason, all roads seemed to lead back to the home of Akley FC. Throughout his life, this place had meant so much to him, and now, at the lowest possible ebb of his life, here he was again. He had stood in this same place when, aged fourteen, Ashley had played his first senior match for the club. He had watched with pride when Ashley had been picked to captain the county under seventeens' side (Ashley was fifteen at the time) and almost shed tears of joy when his boy scored the winning goal.

And now, here he stood again, trying to make sense of it all.

And failing.

The thing about death was there was nothing the living could do to change anything. It wasn't like an accident or illness where there was still hope, sometimes however slim. Death was final. And all the living could do was process it in the best way they could.

This afternoon, a feature came on as he sat half watching the local news on his mother's small television. The reporter stood in front of swathes of flowers and spoke into her microphone. He could hear her saying: '..........local boy, who had been tipped to become a professional footballer but all of that changed on Wednesday night when he was stabbed to death at around seven thirty in the evening......' He stabbed at the remote control and switched the television off.

The words 'all of that changed on Wednesday night' swam round and around in his head. He couldn't concentrate on anything. He didn't know whether to stand up or sit down. It finally dawned on him that he would never see, hear, touch, or feel his son again. This, he supposed, was what true grief felt like.

Jason knew, more than that, was certain that the move to Spain was the right thing to do. He instinctively knew that Holly would get better away from her friends and all the bad influences and temptations they strung out before her.

He knew that in Spain, Ashley would have thrived. He was certain if only he could have got the boy and his mum out there, everything would've been different.

But he also knew that he had underestimated the influence and sheer cruelty of Liz Matthews. She would undermine him at every opportunity. She would play on Holly's insecurities and her uncertainties.

'Jason James wasn't good enough. Spain wasn't like England; you'd hate it, Hol. You're far better off staying here with me where Ashley would have a stable family life. I could take care of him when you, you know, had your periods of being unhappy because, you know, they will come again, they always do.'

Spain hadn't been a bed of roses, that was true, but it was a whole lot better than the alternative. The club were great and stuck to all of its promises. Nice accommodation, a good salary and paid for flights home, within reason, to see Holly and Ashley.

But he missed them terribly, and his mother, whom he was close to. The other lads from the team all had girlfriends and would spend their evenings in their company. Occasionally Jason would get an invite to join some of them, and he would go along. Still, he felt like an outsider looking in at their happiness. He hoped that when Holly got there, he would feel more like part of it all.

The racism was worse than he ever could have imagined. He understood that part of his being given an opportunity was because he was a black player and that it was change that the powers that be were looking for by introducing more black players, but some of the abuse astounded him.

He had never really encountered racism in England. Nothing that he couldn't handle anyway. In matches, some of his more experienced opponents would seek to get a reaction out of him by telling him that he was a 'black bastard' or 'that he should go home with the rest of his kind', but these same blokes would sit with him in the bar after the match and have a drink, a sort of 'no hard feelings' way of looking at things. He could compartmentalise that in his mind, sort of all part of the game, and move on.

But here, even some of his teammates were racist. After one training session, he opened his kit bag and found that someone had placed a bunch of bananas in there. No one owned up. No-one smiled. It clearly wasn't a joke. If it was, no one had found it funny.

The opposition supporters made monkey noises in matches when he received the ball. What hurt more was if he had a bad game, or made a poor pass, the home supporters, his own supporters, would do the same.

It really came to a head when one of his teammates got married, and everyone except Jason was invited to the wedding. The player in question mumbled an apology. It seemed that his fiancée's father, who was paying for everything, didn't like blacks, so he couldn't extend an invitation – he was very sorry.

In the past, Jason always had his father around to discuss these sorts of things. Rationalise them, as it were. His father had seen real racism in his time, and for all the horrible things he was facing, he knew that his father had faced far, far worse in his time.

His father passed away around ten years ago, and Jason found he had lost his adviser, his earth, his person to tell him that everything would be okay. And he had never replaced him.

Things gradually improved in Spain. It seemed that the drive to lessen racism was working to a degree. Jason was pleased for himself, other black players and future black players. If his taking some pain made life easier for those following, then so be it.

But there was still no sign of Holly and Ashley coming out to join him. Jason had asked his friends to watch out for her as best they could, but they all had their own lives to cope with, and watching out for Holly was a major ask; he knew that.

He could feel Holly slipping away from him. Then she announced that she was pregnant again. This time she seemed less keen, less happy, and less optimistic. On the other hand, he saw it as an opportunity. Surely with two children, Holly would see the benefits of living in Spain.

But no. It seemed that Liz Matthews had gotten her claws in deep. Holly made some half-hearted promises about coming out after the baby was born but how it was 'better to have my mum around for the birth'. Jason was so annoyed; he could almost hear Liz Matthews saying those very words.

When the baby was born, what should have been one of their best-shared experiences in life became one of the very worst. Jason wasn't proud of himself, and to this day, he still hated himself for his reaction, but he couldn't help himself. He left the delivery room at the hospital and took a cab to the airport, where he booked himself on the first available flight home.

He made good as best he could. He sent money home and kept up his visits because he wanted to see Ashley, but he couldn't find any love or sympathy for Holly. As far as he was concerned, she had taken his heart and ripped it up in front of him.

Back in Spain, he met someone, and they married pretty quickly. She understood that Ashley was still very much part of his life and accepted his trips home as part and parcel of being with him. They started a family.

The club were promoted in successive seasons and reached the second tier of the Spanish football league. By now, Jason was well into his thirties and aware that his days as a player were numbered. Nevertheless, he did his coaching badges and took on some media work. His Spanish was just about acceptable for local radio. He was doing fine; life was as good as it could be.

But always, at the back of his mind was Ashley; his career was getting close to launch, and when it came, what a launch it was going to be.

And now, nothing. All gone.

After switching off the television report, Jason blindly made his way back to the club, and in particular, his favourite spot.

This was where he felt safest. This is where he felt at home.

Chapter Nineteen

Saturday 14th November – 15:35

Davey Mcniven was very much a creature of habit.

Today he was on duty in the tea hut on the far side of the ground. When he first did tea hut duty, under the guiding hand of his mother, she told him that he should get to the ground an hour and a half before the scheduled kick-off and, using the giant tea caddy, boil up 7 pints of water. That way, when the first supporters arrived fifteen minutes before kick-off, he would be ready to dispense them cups of steaming hot tea.

That was what he had done today.

However, when he scanned what he could see of the ground from the open-sided hut, he could make out only five, maybe six people, in attendance. That meant a pint of tea for each of them – if they wanted.

He knew there would be very few people at the ground today before he arrived two and a quarter hours ago. Of course, the constant rain always meant that attendance would be poor, but still, he turned up an hour and a half early, and still, he boiled seven points of water. He wondered why he did that – probably because his mother told him. He had never considered changing that, no matter what the circumstances.

He was a compliant individual. He always did what he was told without question. He felt that other people knew better, and were more intelligent than he was, so why would he ever doubt what they told him?

One person he could make out through the haze rising from the wet grass was Jason James, standing in his usual spot behind the crash barrier at the river end. He hadn't moved since the game kicked off. Even though the rain lashed into him, he stood, stock still, staring into space.

If Mcniven had the wherewithal to feel pity, then he would do so.

Jason James had been a close friend back in the day. They joined the club on the same day, aged seven, and were best friends. Jason was a far superior footballer but Mcniven, and he remained very close. When Jason was released from the professional club he had been at since the age of, what, nine or ten, it was Mcniven who he chose to spend the most time with. It was Mcniven whose company he sought in the most desperate hours of his young life.

Mcniven knew as an individual; he did not offer much. He wasn't insightful; he wasn't fun; he wasn't interesting. He was none of the things that made people charismatic.

What he did offer was loyalty. He was loyal, dependable, and reliable. That, he guessed, was what Jason James saw in him.

When Jason went to Spain, Mcniven was genuinely pleased for him. He knew he would miss him dearly, but

Jason's life had moved on. He had Holly and, not long after, Ashley. His life had taken a new direction. Mcniven's had stagnated, but that was fine. His parents had moved away, but he now had one-bedroom flat. He had a steady, if unexciting, job at the local supermarket, which paid him what he needed, but mostly he had Akley FC. Whenever he wasn't working or sleeping, he was usually at the club doing one of those jobs that always needed to be done.

He was known to some members, in a kindhearted way, as 'Mr Akley'. And when he thought about it, that is what he was 'Mr Akley'.

None of this gave him much time to make new friends and relationships. He supposed that he became a bit reclusive, a bit introspective.

With Jason spending three out of every four weeks away, he asked Mcniven to watch out for Holly. Mcniven knew Holly and very much liked her. He saw her and Jason as a very good union. Still, he knew from conversations with Jason that she was vulnerable. So, he was happy to help out his good friend.

Regrettably, it was a task that proved too much for Mcniven to handle. It was beyond his skill set, both physically and mentally. Moreover, Holly's problems ran far deeper than Mcniven could ever have imagined. Although he tried, Holly's resolve was far greater than he had ever had to deal with before. The bottom line was that if Holly wanted something, Holly got it.

Mcniven knew she was seeing her old friends, but his loyalty to her this time got in the way. Every time he spoke to Jason and Jason asked how things were going, Mcniven always said fine; they seemed fine.

But they weren't. Holly was savvy enough to get her act together every time Jason came home, but as soon as he was on the plane to Spain, she was out again with her friends.

It came to a head when she fell pregnant again, and the baby was born. Jason was crushed.

Clearly, the child wasn't his.

And that changed everything. Three relationships – Mcniven and Jason, Jason and Holly and Holly and Mcniven – would never be the same again.

So much for loyalty, thought Mcniven. It's overrated.

Chapter Twenty

Saturday 14th November – 22:45

It was just like the opening scene of *The Godfather*.

The room was dark, with only two shaded lamps on either side of the vast mahogany desk giving out any light, and even that was aimed downwards. The floor was carpeted, and there were bookcases along the walls. Even though the room was reasonably sized, it felt claustrophobic. Jamieson sat in a leather chair facing Tony Di Angelo, who was behind the desk. Hess was seated against the back wall and to Jamieson's left - a bit like his wingman - Jamieson could not see Hes unless he turned his head almost one hundred and eighty degrees. Jamieson could not help but feel this was by design. Di Angelo's father and adviser, Bruno, stood behind him with his hands crossed behind his back, his head bowed down in apparent deference to his son.

The only thing that seemed misplaced was the repeated thump, thump of the bass line from the music being played in the club downstairs.

An hour earlier, Jamieson had been sitting at home waiting for Match of the Day to start. His mobile rang, and he answered. It was Hess.

'Do you want the good news first or the bad news?' He asked, then: 'Actually scrap that; I'm going with the good news first. Di Angelo wants to meet with you.'

'OK,' Said Jamieson ', when?'

'In about half an hour at his club.'

Jamieson checked his watch: ten-fifteen on a Saturday evening.

Hess continued: 'I think it'll be worth your while. The Don doesn't grant too many audiences, so he will have something important to your case......'

'Ok', said Jamieson ', let's do it.'

They arranged for Hess to pick Jamieson up and drive him into town for the meeting. Jamieson went upstairs to find Lucy and explain what was happening. Lucy wasn't fazed; she knew the life of a policeman wasn't exactly nine to five: 'Just you take care,' she said and kissed him on the cheek. 'I'll see you later - don't wake me up if I'm asleep!'

On the drive over, Hess explained more about gang life in Bedfordshire and how the pecking order began with The Dons, followed a bit further back by Danny Mack's gang L6, and then the rest a fair way back. It was understood that nobody did anything without approaching Di Angelo first and receiving his blessing.

The Dons was formed in the seventies by Tony's old man, Bruno. It was an effective unit, but ,it reached an altogether higher plain when Tony took over. Tony was degree educated in business studies and carried that ethos into gang life.

When they reached the Di Angelo club, the security team had cordoned off parking for Hess. He pulled in and parked.

Jamieson stepped out of the car and viewed the outside of the club. There was a significant queue of Millennials waiting to get in. Funny, their evening was starting as Jamieson's would have been close to finishing. He supposed there was a time when his nights out were like that - only he couldn't recall when.

Hess moved ahead, and Jamieson tugged him back by the arm: 'Is this operation all legit?' he asked, indicating the club with an incline of his head.

'It's a bonafide nightclub', Hess replied. 'In that people pay to get in, buy drinks, dance and do whatever else people do in nightclubs. Di Angelo will not allow any drug dealing inside. That is done offsite and by Di Angelo's dealers solely. They might use the club to launder some of the drug money. Still, even that is getting more difficult now because most people use debit cards. So they must be creative and find other ways and methods to get around that.'

When they reached the door, Hes turned to Alex: 'Remember you're here because of your case and what Di Angelo can bring to the table for that. So don't worry about anything else; that's my domain.'

They were ushered through the club's foyer and spotted disappointed punters being turned away by overzealous doormen. Groups of males didn't stand a chance. Jamieson had spotted some desperate horse trading going on further back in the queue between groups of blokes and groups of girls in an attempt to turn groups into couples and then back to groups once inside.

Hess led them to a door. He knocked, and it was opened immediately. They were expected. Security pointed them up the stairs. They were met by another burly-shaven-headed heavy who knocked at another door and went inside. He came out almost immediately and ushered them through.

Di Angelo spoke for the first time: 'Inspector Jamieson, good evening; Hess here tells me that you have been put in charge of the case involving the young boy who was knifed up on Rankin Avenue last week. That was a terrible, terrible tragedy indeed.'

Jamieson nodded: "Firstly, Mr Di Angelo, thank you for your time and help. I appreciate that you are a busy man, and, yes, a young man losing his life in that manner is a tragic event.'

Di Angelo made a steeple with the fingers of each hand and placed his elbows on the desk in front of him: 'How can I help you?' he asked.

Jamieson thought how best to frame his words: 'There is a rumour that the boy, Ashley James, was working in some capacity for you. He had come into some significant sums of money of late, and we're looking at how that may have been.'

Di Angelo nodded for what felt like an age: 'You will understand that I am not acquainted with all the people associated with the organisation. I have, however, spoken to some of my Capos, my most trusted men, and they have confirmed that the boy in question did some work for us.'

'Can you elaborate for us, Mr Di Angelo?' asked Jamieson.

Di Angelo picked up a bottle of mineral water on the table and unscrewed the lid. He pointed it towards Jamieson: 'Can I pour one for you, Inspector?' he asked.

'Thank you', replied Jamieson.

As quick as a flash, Bruno was at his son's side with two cut glass crystal glasses. He poured two glasses. A satisfying glug, glug as the sparkling water fell into each glass broke the immediate silence - the beat from downstairs went on.

Di Angelo took a mouthful and nodded appreciatively: 'Nice', he said. Jamieson raised his glass in salute and took a mouthful of his own.

Di Angelo took a deep breath: 'He turned up one evening with David Macklin's son. David Macklin had asked me to consider using his son within the organisation. I said yes because Macklin Senior is in construction, which I thought might be useful at some point. But the son.....' He made the very Italian gesture of index finger to thumb and a gentle shake of the hand '....what can I say? He was an idiot. If brains were dynamite, he wouldn't have enough to blow his nose.'

'You see, Inspector, in our business, it's not about bragging and acting the big man, which is what the fool did. We don't want to draw attention to what we do, and our clients don't want us to do that either. So we work quietly and without fuss, perhaps 'under the radar'. Macklin junior didn't understand that, and we politely informed him that we wouldn't need his services any longer.'

He continued: 'Young James, on the other hand.... very intelligent, very perceptive. Got it straight away. Proved to be an excellent link between ourselves and the end user. After a month or so, he sought out his Capo and told him that he needed to earn good money and quickly, it seemed his Mother had frittered away the rent money. The family were about to be evicted, so the Capo moved him away from the users who spent fifty or a hundred pounds from their welfare cheques to, shall we say, our more lucrative clients.'

'What might he earn in a week, say?' asked Jamieson.

Di Angelo spread his hands in front of him: 'Well, for, shall we say, our standard users, he would have been expected to do ten drops in an evening and earn fifty pounds for that.'

'But for our 'special' clients, well, they tip well, and we give half to the courier. We have a lot of special clients, and they spend well and frequently - without going into too much detail, we have pop stars, music producers, film producers, and actors, but the best payers are the city boys, the traders. Those boys earn so much money they have lost all understanding of value. As long as they've got stuff to shovel up their noses, they don't care what they are paying for it - not that we inflate the price too much, they're not stupid, and they could easily shop around - if they want to push an extra fifty or a hundred into the courier's hand for the service, well that's up to them.'

Suddenly it was easy for Jamieson to see where Ashley James had come into the levels of money that he had. Even if he only worked Friday and Saturday evenings picking up a minimum of two hundred and fifty each evening, that was around two thousand pounds a month. That sort of money would easily make inroads into the rent arrears and enable young Ashley to keep on top of living expenses and give his brothers and sisters treats such as expensive trainers that he thought they deserved.

'On the night he died, was Ashley working for you?' asked Jamieson.

Di Angelo thought about his answer: 'He was on his way to meet his Capo. One of the other couriers had let us down, and Ashley had stepped in at short notice. He wasn't on his way to a drop-off, nor was he on his way back from a drop-off.'

Again, Jamieson found himself framing his next question very carefully: 'Do you believe that there is any way that the events of that evening had anything to do with what he had become involved in?'

Di Angelo considered his answer: 'I cannot give you a hundred per cent guarantee, but, honestly, I don't think so.'

He continued: 'Hess will have told you that particular road where Ashley was found is shared between ourselves and L6s. Danny Mack used to work for me a few years ago. He had a lot of similarities to Ashley James - intelligent, focused, driven - I guess you could say he was my protégée. He asked me if he could start up independently, and I gave him my blessing. We have a very cordial working relationship. Danny knows how I work and has cloned it for his own working method. We have a mutual respect for each other's businesses.'

'I have spoken with Danny. When things like this happen on the patch where you work, it brings problems. It brings police; it brings reporters asking questions; it brings television cameras. None of these things is good for business. We want to fly under the radar where no one will notice what we are doing.'

'Danny and I have spoken to our capos, who have spoken to their soldiers. There is no indication that this is anything to do with gang warfare. I don't believe an outside gang would dare to step onto Dons' territory. That would be seen as an act of gang war, and no-one wants to take The Dons on. We would simply crush them.'

The beat from downstairs filled the silence.

Chapter Twenty-One

Saturday 14th November – 23:10

Chief Constable Peter Jarman rolled off Detective Sergeant Claire Evason. He lay beside her, his breathing quick, his chest rising and falling.

Immediately Evason covered herself with a sheet. A strange reaction given that she had just been as intimate as you could be with another person, but the second that intimacy had finished, her sense of decency and morality would kick in.

On the other hand, Jarman had no such problem with his sense of decorum. He lay naked. Evason scanned him out of the corner of her eye - close-cropped hair, muscular shoulders, flat stomach, his spent penis lying flat amidst a forest of pubic hair.

His breathing returned to normal, and he reached out and touched her forearm. She thought for a moment he was going to shake her hand and say, 'Excellent Detective Sergeant, textbook intercourse.'

Instead, he rolled toward the bedside table and picked up his phone. 'Christ, is that the time?' he said, pushing himself off the bed and heading towards the bathroom. 'I really need to get going.'

Evason heard the shower start up.

This was Evason's private life, and up to now, it had very much been her choice.

She had met Jarman at a policing event where he was the keynote speaker - corporate speak - she had found him captivating, charming and charismatic. She couldn't remember, per se, what he had said, but moreover, the way he had said it, the way he moved about the stage, the confidence he conveyed to the audience.

After, in the bar, Evason broke the rule of a lifetime and sought Jarman out. He was seated amongst some senior police hierarchy from around the country. Still, she confidently edged into the group and, more importantly, into the seat next to Jarman. They talked long and hard into the evening. Gradually members of their group moved away; however, so intense was their conversation that it wasn't until just after midnight that they realised they were the remaining two people in the bar.

Emboldened by alcohol, Evason broke her second rule of a lifetime of the evening.

'You can take me to bed if you like.' she said, not quite believing what she had just said aloud.

Jarman looked at her through his alcohol-induced haze. He took his mobile phone from his pocket: 'What's your number?' He asked.

As she told him, he pressed the digits on his handset. Evason heard her phone ring in her shoulder bag. Jarman almost immediately hung up.

'Save my number, and if you ever want anything in the future, call me. I will always be delighted to hear from you.' He smiled: 'You are beautiful, you are intelligent, and you are very, very drunk. I will walk you to your room, say goodnight, and ensure you are safely inside. Then I will go to my room, and we'll both have a good night's sleep and see what tomorrow brings.'

The following morning Evason slept through her alarm and missed the first lecture of the day, ironically called 'Alcohol and the workings of the criminal mind'.

Her head was heavy, but she eventually hauled herself out of bed and showered. She got downstairs at ten past ten only to find out that breakfast finished at ten o'clock. A sympathetic waiter offered to put together a plate of food from the buffet, which had disappeared back into the kitchen. While she was waiting, Evason helped herself to a black coffee from a nearby machine.

While her cup was filling, she was joined by another delegate from the course.

'Many in there?' she asked, indicating the hall with a dip of her head.

'Quite empty,' came the reply ', it seems that something big happened overnight, so most of the top brass have been recalled to their areas to deal with it.'

She felt a wave of disappointment wash over her. Top brass almost certainly included Jarman.

She sat at a nearby table, sipped her coffee, and picked at the plate of food. She thought about last evening.

He turned her down.

She had thrown herself at him, and he turned her down.

She didn't know whether to be angry; 'What was wrong with her? Didn't he find her attractive? Christ, she had offered herself on a plate, and he'd said 'no thanks'. What was wrong with him more like?!!'

She didn't know whether to be grateful; She'd acted impetuously, impulsively; that was not her style at all. He'd said no because he respected her, knew that it was the alcohol speaking, and knew that she would regret things in the morning.

She pulled her mobile from her shoulder bag and looked at the call log. Last night's missed call sat there. She opened her contacts list and saved the number under the cryptic entry 'P'.

The rest of the day dragged on. Another time the seminars might have fired up her imagination, but today her mind repeatedly returned to last evening. She had a feeling in the pit of her stomach, which gnawed away. She needed to see this man again. She didn't know why, but she just did.

Finally, the course finished at four o'clock. She collected her bag from the luggage room and found her car. She was ready to pull away when her phone pinged with an incoming text message: 'How's the head?'

It had come from 'P'. Her heart lurched.

They embarked upon an affair. He told her upfront that he was married and that that would not change. She said that was fine. She didn't want anything too serious. Her career was paramount, and nothing should get in the way of that.

She felt bad for the wife - her name was Marion - but she couldn't help herself. There was this compulsion, this drive, whenever she and Jarman were together. Nothing else mattered. Then when they were apart, she hated herself and vowed that it must stop. And then it would happen again. And again.

She never asked Jarman for anything. Initially, he would mention upcoming jobs that would help with her career progression, but she soon put a stop to that. This is not what that was about. Her career was in her own hands - but thanks for asking!

This was around eighteen months ago, and Clare Evason thought she had everything on track. They would meet up a couple of times a month, specifically when Jarman's commitments would allow. Sometimes for a meal and a chat, and other times they would check into a hotel and share a double bed. No ties. It was what both parties wanted.

Then three months ago, Evason's plans took a hammer blow.

An old university friend had given birth and had invited her over for coffee and 'to meet the new addition'. Evason balked at the idea. She didn't want to 'meet the new addition', which actually sounded like her friend had bought a dog. Finally, she ran out of excuses and made arrangements to go over one Saturday for an hour, but no more, because 'I know how busy it must be with a young child'. She didn't, and also, she didn't really care.

When she arrived, her friend explained that Sebastian was coming around from his afternoon nap and was ready for his feed.

Evason sat with a Nespresso cappuccino balanced on her lap while the friend got Sebastian. When she returned, she said, 'Claire, pop your coffee on the table there and have a hold while I go and get his bottle ready.'

Evason put her cup on the table, and Sebastian was plopped on her lap. The friend disappeared.

Evason gazed down at this tiny package she had been left in charge of. In truth, Sebastian didn't do very much. He yawned, stretched, reached out, held her finger, and went back to sleep.

Bam.

All at once, non-maternal, career-minded, 'who wants to be a Mother?' Claire Evason reached a decision - she wanted one of these.

Her actual natural instincts had taken over against all that she thought were her natural instincts. Of course, this wasn't part of the plan, but plans changed.

Jarman appeared at the door to the bathroom, one towel wrapped around his waist and another around his shoulders.

'I know you don't like this, but an old mate of mine is looking for a DS to work out of the Marylebone station. Always good to get the Met on your CV. It puts you in good stead for when you start looking for your first Detective Inspector role. Just saying.....' He held his hands up in mock surrender.

Evason gave a tired smile: 'Okay, I'll think about it.' Then she changed tack. 'Did you know Alex Jamieson played guitar in a covers band?'

Jarman raised his eyebrows and shook his head: 'A man of many talents clearly.' He pulled on his underwear and looked around for his socks.

Evason continued, 'They're playing a charity gig on 11th December. He's put out an open invite. I wondered whether you would like to go. Obviously, we can't go to-gether, but there is no reason why we shouldn't attend as part of a workgroup. Sounds like it could be good fun.'

Jarman tied his laces: 'Sounds good. Send me a text, and I'll put it in my diary. We can make our excuses early and sneak away somewhere, perhaps.'

He stood and picked up his jacket, shrugging into it until the fit felt right. Then, finally, he picked up his briefcase.

'You may as well stay the night; nice hotel, one of the perks of the job.' He leant forward and kissed her on the forehead. 'See you soon. Take care.'

As the door closed behind him, Evason knew she had much thinking to do. She got out of bed and went into the bathroom. She wouldn't be staying tonight. She wasn't sure if she hadn't become a perk of the job as well.

Chapter Twenty-Two

Sunday 15th November – 00:45

When it came to Jamieson's job, Lucy always acted very relaxed, and most of the time, she was. If she had been on tenterhooks the whole time he was working, the relationship would have disintegrated years ago. However, in times of doubt, which she would admit were seldom, she wondered where she stood in the pecking order of Jamieson's obligations.

She would have been wrong if she ever thought policing came above her. As much as Jamieson loved his work, he loved Lucy a million times greater.

However, tonight Lucy felt nervous. It was one thing for Jamieson to get up and go to work at seven in the morning but entirely different when he receives a call after ten on a Saturday evening for a meeting involving murder, potentially, anyway.

What sort of individuals had meetings at that time of the day? Gangsters? Drug dealers? Murderers?

So, she was putting on an act when she kissed him and told him not to wake her up when he got in. She would not be sleeping from when he left until she heard his door key in the lock. Then she would turn off the bedside light and make out that she had been asleep since he had left earlier.

They had met some twenty-five years earlier at university. Jamieson had been very drunk, and Lucy very sober. Jamieson had acted like a goon. He had been drinking with his rugby friends, and to impress them (or perhaps, more accurately, Lucy), he had joined a local band on stage. It had ended in disaster, with him falling off the stage and returning to the group to hoots of derision.

At the end of the evening, he asked her for her number. She had said 'no, but she would meet him for breakfast at eight-thirty the following morning in the cafe opposite the university.'

That would test his resolve. It was now well past midnight, and he was horribly drunk, eight thirty would be a real challenge.

'I'll be there.' Announced Jamieson, slurring his words and giving her a thumbs up and a big drunken grin.

And he was.

Ok, he was wearing the same clothes as the evening before and smelt a bit of stale booze and cigarettes, but he was there.

Lucy was impressed. She looked closely at him sitting opposite her. He was a bit green around the gills, and she suspected he was still drunk. Still, he had a nice face and lovely eyes topped off with a slightly wild, floppy mop of black hair (we'll do something about that, she thought to herself).

She let him off the hook. She scribbled her number on a scrap of paper and handed it to him:

'Go home.' She said, 'Go to bed. I'm free on Wednesday evening. Call me, and we can go out then.'

Jamieson raised a finger: 'No, no, I'm f..........'

Lucy grabbed his finger and lowered his hand to the table: 'Yes, yes.' She said. 'You've got my number; you've got your date. So, if I were you, I'd quit while I was ahead.'

'You're sure?' asked Jamieson.

'I'm sure', replied Lucy.

Jamieson called on Monday evening and arranged to meet on Wednesday evening at seven. The plan was to grab a quick drink and then go to the cinema. The suggested films were Jumanji (Lucy) or Se7en (Jamieson). They would decide on the night.

As it was, they never made the cinema. Instead, they settled into a quiet area of the pub and spent their time chatting. By the time Jamieson checked his watch, both of the chosen films had started.

Jamieson apologised for his behaviour on Saturday evening. Lucy said no problem. They talked about where they were from, She, Stevenage, in Hertfordshire, and he, Ealing, in West London. They spoke of their families: Lucy had an older brother, Simon, and Jamieson had a younger sister, Joanne. Both sets of parents were still around and still together. They talked about their university courses. He was in his final year studying geography, and she was in her second year studying marketing and advertising. He told her he intended to join the police force when he left in the summer. He needed a 2:1, and he was on schedule. That meant he could enter the force on an accelerated programme and make detective earlier than the traditional route. She could see he was passionate about this, and she warmed to him even more. She liked passion; what could she say?

Their second date was on the Saturday, and they saw Se7en, not the most romantic of films, but to this day, Lucy still smiled when she saw it being shown on television.

On their fifth date, they slept together for the first time, a bit sooner than Lucy would have liked, but they had been out for a meal and enjoyed a couple of bottles of wine, and she was caught up in the moment. And besides, she knew it would happen sooner or later anyway, so sooner was not a real problem.

In the summer, Jamieson graduated, having secured his required 2:1 and went through the selection process for the accelerated detective programme. He was selected and was due to begin in October. That meant they had the summer to themselves. They spent June and July working hard to build up some cash, and then for the whole of August, they inter-railed through Europe. They took in Paris (romantic), Berlin (historical), Amsterdam (grown-up), Rome (disappointing, must go back and give it a second chance), and Madrid (Cultured), amongst other places, staying in the cheapest accommodation they could find, usually youth hostels.

They grew closer and closer, and it was no surprise to anyone when Jamieson proposed to Lucy on her graduation day the following summer. He wasn't one for spontaneity, so he had asked her beforehand what, if, in the case of him, maybe, perhaps, asking her to marry him, what would she say? She still liked to tease him gently, so she told him 'probably', and he would have to make do with that.

Being a traditionalist, Jamieson travelled to Stevenage to ask Lucy's parents for her hand in marriage. Lucy's father, Stan, was a decent man, but Jamieson struggled to get the words out. They talked about everything under the sun, including the plants in the back garden. Finally, Stan sat Jamieson down and gave him a small whiskey.

'Son', he said, 'I can see you've got something important to ask me, and I'm pretty sure I know what it is. The answer will be in your favour, so ask away.'

Jamieson gulped the whiskey and took a deep breath: 'I love your daughter very much, and I would like your permission to ask her to marry me, please.' It came out as a splurge, but he had done it.

Stan smiled and slapped Jamieson on the shoulder. 'Son,' he said, 'I couldn't think of a more suitable and caring bloke to pass her onto. You have my blessing many times over.'

They married in the summer of nineteen ninety-six and moved to Flitwick in Bedfordshire, close to Lucy's parents but still within striking distance of Ealing, where Jamieson's folks were. Jamieson had his first posting as a Detective Sergeant in Milton Keynes. Lucy also had a job in Milton Keynes. She put her Honours Degree into good use by working for a small marketing company specialising in the medical sector.

In late ninety-eight, Alexander William Jamieson - Xander - was born. Three years later, Justin came along.

In a nice symmetry, Xander was now at Birmingham University, where Lucy and Jamieson first met. Justin was in the first year of sixth form, preparing for his A-levels. The two boys got on well. As hard as Xander had to work, Justin found everything in life to be pretty straightforward. He would be going to university as well but knowing him, he would avoid Birmingham to buck the trend.

Lucy went back to part-time employment after the birth of each son. Jamieson's career continued upward, and he reached the height of Detective Inspector at the relatively youthful age of thirty-five. In his own words, he had stalled since, but he told himself that was because other, more essential issues had gotten in the way.

Lucy lay awake. She had read five chapters of a pretty uninspiring novel and then put it down. She had watched a couple of episodes of a drama that she enjoyed on her tablet. Still, it couldn't quite hold her interest like it usually did.

Finally, at a quarter to one, she heard a car pull up outside and muffled voices. The car pulled away again, and she heard the sound of a key in the lock.

She turned out the bedside light and rolled under the covers. She could relax for now. He was home again.

Chapter Twenty-Three

Sunday 15th November – 10:15

Claire Evason stretched out her long legs with her arms pushing way above her head. Her back arched, and she let out a loud groan.

There was nothing like your own bed, and although she would have to make do with muesli and toast for breakfast instead of a hotel full English, she was sure she had made the right decision last night.

She looked at the bedside clock - ten thirty - maybe she would go out and treat herself to brunch somewhere.

She felt a little bit grubby as if she had checked in and out of a hotel which let its rooms by the hour, but what could she do about that now?

So, decision time for the day ahead.

She would do an online yoga session in front of the television and then go out for brunch. She wondered if her old university friend was around, or more specifically. She wondered whether she could go and have her regular dose of Sebastian. She smiled when she thought about him; she would ring and see if her friend was free.

She put on her yoga gear, leggings and a t-shirt and went downstairs. She cued up the yoga session through her phone to play on the television and went to the kitchen to fill her water bottle.

With her yoga mat unfurled, she began her session. Fifteen minutes in, and in the middle of a downward-facing dog, her phone rang, breaking her relaxed state of mind. She paused the session and looked at the number. It wasn't one she recognised, but she answered anyway.

'DS Evason, ' she answered.

'This is Mrs Matthews. Is that the woman policeman who came round yesterday?'

'Yes, Mrs Matthews, I am. What can I do for you?' Evason was wary but polite.

'Holly is still in bed, so she doesn't know I'm calling, but I wanted to tell you that Jason James was around Friday. Asking lots of questions and putting pressure on Holly, blaming her for what happened, said she should have looked after Ash better. He got her in a right state when it was his fault; for God's sake, he left her. He knew she wasn't up to looking after herself, let alone four kids. He makes my blood boil, bastard that he is.'

'Ok, Mrs Matthews', said Evason. 'Did things get physical at all? Or were they just talking?'

'Just talking. He's far too smart to lose his rag and do anything that might get him into trouble, but I'll tell you this, he's got a temper on him; that man has. I've seen him raise a fist to Holly before now. Holly told him about seeing that Macklin lad, and he got really annoyed about that. Starting 'effing and blinding about what he was gonna do to him and all that. He's a wrong 'un, he is'

'Ok, Mrs Matthews, thanks for letting us know. Perhaps if he comes round in future, it would be best not to let him in and just call us instead.' Evason said.

'I will do that', replied the big woman. 'I tell you, I just don't trust that man.' And with that, she was gone.

Evason tapped her phone gently against her teeth while she pondered the contents of the call. She couldn't work out whether that was genuine motherly concern or whether she had just been played like a fiddle.

Lucy made Jamieson breakfast in bed. Egg, bacon, beans, two slices of toast, and a big mug of tea.

Jamieson stretched and let out a groan.

'What's this in aid of?' he asked. 'I don't usually qualify for breakfast in bed.'

Lucy placed the tray in his lap, leaned forward, and kissed his forehead: 'Think yourself lucky then.' Then, she said, 'What time did you get home last night?'

'Think it was around one', replied Jamieson, liberally applying ketchup to his breakfast. 'This looks lovely, by the way.'

'What do you want to do today?' asked Lucy, looking out the window. 'It is still, quite literally, lashing down with rain.'

Jamieson thought, through a mouthful of egg and bacon, he said: 'We could wrap up against the elements and go for a long walk ending in a pub for Sunday lunch,' he suggested ', or I could finish this lovely breakfast, and you could come back to bed, and we could see what happens?' he said, an innocent look on his face.

Lucy thought: 'A long walk and lunch sound nice.' She said.

The look of utter dismay on Jamieson's face made her face crease into a huge grin before she stripped off her dressing gown and slid into bed next to him. He wolfed down the rest of his breakfast before she changed her mind.

Stone was up and getting ready to go into the office. That's what he did at the weekend, almost precisely what he did during the week.

Today, however, he had a spring in his step. He, Pete Stone, nearing his mid-fifties, had been asked out by, from memory, a very attractive woman. But, with everything going on around the situation that he and Margaret had found themselves in, he felt a bit battered and worthless, as if he had nothing to offer anyone, let alone someone he found attractive.

So, in short, today, Sandy was buzzing. He had saved Helen's number in his contacts and would call her back. He would call her back, not just at the moment but soon, he would call her back. Definitely, he would.

Johnson was also having a good day.

Yesterday evening after playing rugby, he had met up with his brother for a few beers and a meal, not a curry; Steve didn't like Indian, so they were sitting in a steak house, which Steve liked best. In truth, even Johnson would admit the food was good. They were chatting when the waiter bought their desserts across - Steve had tiramisu and Johnson key lime pie - At the beginning of the evening, the waiter, a gentle-looking soul with the darkest eyes Johnson had ever seen, had introduced himself as David and shown them to their table. David and Johnson had been gently flirting throughout the meal.

'Lovely eyes.' said Johnson.

'Who?' replied Steve.

'David, the waiter.' answered Johnson.

'Not noticed.' said Steve, then after what felt like a life-time, 'Is he gay then?' He genuinely meant the question.

'Yes,' said Johnson ', he's gay.'

'How do you know that then?' asked Steve.

'Don't you know we've all got a 'G' tattooed on our fore-heads', laughed Johnson. 'You really do live up to your billing as the straightest man in the world, don't you?'

Steve grinned back and shrugged; 'Can't help it.' he said, 'You gonna go for it?' He smiled, gesturing towards David with his forehead.

Johnson smiled back. He held up the restaurant business card that the waiter had placed on the table before him when he left the desserts. He flipped it over. On the back, it said: 'David' followed by a phone number.

'What can I say?' said Johnson, shrugging nonchalantly.

'Bloody marvellous', said Steve.

Chapter Twenty-Four

Sunday 15th November – 14:00

This was part of the week that didn't do anything for either Max Allen or Alison Fairly.

They both enjoyed the daily buzz of paramedic life - neither minded shift work - they both found that the busier they were, the quicker time passed.

They knew that the job came with good days and bad days - sometimes your actions would save a life; other days, whatever your actions, a life may be lost.

Max was in his early forties and had fifteen years in the job. He had never intended to make a career out of being a paramedic, but inertia kicked in, and he was always on the verge of a change without it ever actually happening. He was married with two kids and a mortgage. Deep down, he knew he would still be in the job in another twenty years. By then, he may have moved off the vans, as paramedics called them, into a managerial role. However, he would still be wearing the green uniform either way.

Alison Fairly was thirty-nine. She was late to the service, having originally trained as a teacher and raising two kids. They were now in their early teens and had become almost self-sufficient. Alison's husband, Jim, had taken up with a girl in her early twenties a couple of years ago, and Alison decided it was time to reinvent herself. She needed a vocation, and a paramedic role suited her perfectly. She was fortunate that her Mother lived close by and was always happy to be there for the kids when Alison had to work a night shift.

Alison had been a fully trained paramedic for just over a year and particularly enjoyed working shifts with Max.

Alison enjoyed the banter with Max. Max often said things that went as far as the line, but never did he overstep. Alison felt safe with him. He looked out for her and made sure she was always okay. Alison thought she was a little bit in love with Max but knew that was as far as it could ever go. Max was always talking about his wife, Emma.

Once each week, the paramedic pairings had to start their shift an hour early. This was to allow them to give their 'van' a thorough clean-out. There was a daily, end-of-shift, clean but, because each van was constantly used twenty-four hours a day, this was perhaps best described as perfunctory. A van off the road was not considered the best use of NHS assets.

So today, Sunday 15th November, was Max and Alison's day to give Cindy, the name they had given to their van, a thorough clean-out.

Max lowered the tailgate and wheeled the trolly out onto the forecourt.

'So, what did you get up to last night?' he asked Alison.

Alison was disinfecting the van inside: 'Strictly,' she said. It was amazing how one word could sum up a Saturday evening.

'Any good?' Said Max.

'Not sure I like the celebrities this season,' answered Alison. 'Too many reality people.'

They worked in silence for the next ten minutes or so.

'Oh, hello.' said Alison suddenly.

Max looked across. She was bending over and reaching into the corner of the van. He looked at her figure for a little bit too long, which, even in the green, unflattering paramedic outfit, he had always found pleasing to the eye. Then, he snapped out of it: 'What have you found?' he asked.

Alison reversed out. Max could see she was holding a mobile phone in her rubber-gloved right hand between her index finger and thumb. Max could see that the screen had been bashed in.

'Shoved right into the corner, underneath the oxygen tank. Looks like someone didn't want it found.' She said.

'Stick it in a plastic bag and hand it in to control', Said Max. 'They'll have to go through the manifest for the last week, see if they can work out who left it behind.' He smiled: 'Good find.' He said.

Alison set off across the forecourt towards control. She loved Max's smile. Yes, she was a little bit in love with him.

Max watched Alison move away and shook his head: 'It'll soon be the Christmas party.' he thought ', I need to be on my best behaviour that night.'

Chapter Twenty-Five

Sunday 15th November – 23:15

Michael Macklin just did not see it coming.

It was eleven fifteen, and he was just leaving the pub, having been there since six thirty. He had started on pints of strong lager and did shots with a group of like-minded drinkers by the pool table.

Michael Macklin sober was a nasty piece of work. Michael Macklin drunk was everyone's worse nightmare.

On the way out, he lurched into a table, spilling drinks; 'Sorry, sorry', he slurred.

'Be careful.' Said a middle-aged woman who had been enjoying a night out with friends.

'Fuck off, you cow,' replied Macklin.

He crashed through the door onto the street outside and staggered towards home, bouncing off hedges and walls as he went.

Halfway home, he realised he needed to relieve himself, so he unzipped and pissed where he stood in the middle of the pavement.

The first blow came as Macklin shook himself off and zipped up.

It sounded very much like a wooden baseball bat. It made a pleasing 'thunk' as it bounced off the back of Macklin's head.

Despite his young age, Macklin was a big bastard and didn't go down. He staggered forward, eventually found his footing and stood, albeit unsteadily, where he was for a good ten seconds trying to make sense of what had happened.

Finally, he turned around.

Before he got all the way around, the second blow came in. This one was equally pleasing and more effective. It caught Macklin on the left cheekbone. Teeth flew from his mouth; blood spurted from his nose.

Macklin dropped to his knees.

The third, but by no means the final blow, was another to the back of the head, a bit like a full-blooded drive with a golf club. This time Macklin pitched forward. His pulpy, bloodied face crashed into the paving slab. His front two teeth snapped on impact and ended up mixed in with blood, snot and saliva just to the left of his bruised and busted face.

Chapter Twenty-Six

Monday 16th November – 07:25

If you had told Alex Jamieson that three significant factors in the case would occur within the next three hours, it is unlikely that he would have believed you. That sort of thing does not happen in murder cases, not very often, anyway.

Jamieson was driving to work. The meeting with Tony Di Angelo on Saturday evening was to the forefront of his mind. He took Di Angelo very much at face value. There was no reason why he should not. Everything the man said was valid and made sense. It also echoed the comments made by the Cardiff University student when they met on Friday morning.

Successful gangs and Di Angelo ran a very success-ful gang, were functional by nature. However, they were not successful despite themselves. It took hard work and meticulous planning for them to survive and thrive. A key component was the ability to work as far off the grid as possible. 'Under the radar' as Di Angelo himself put it. There would be no benefit in courting the kind of publicity that comes with a murder, particularly a knife-related murder of an adolescent on your doorstep.

So, if not gang-related, then what?

While Jamieson mulled it over, his phone rang. He checked the clock on the dashboard- seven-thirty.

Little did he know it, but this was the first significant factor coming through.

He leant forward and pressed the answer button on the dashboard display: 'DI Jamieson, ' he said.

'Alex, it's Steve Paige from serious incidents here.'

Jamieson knew Paige fleetingly. Reputationally he was held in high regard by his peers.

'Steve', said Jamieson. 'How are you?'

'Good, good', replied Paige. 'I think I have some news of a person of interest in your enquiry. Does the name Michael Macklin ring a bell?'

Jamieson let out a short sharp laugh: 'Yes. Yes,' He said, 'I'd like to say that he's a nice guy, but I would be lying. So what's he been up to?'

'Well, currently, he's lying in the critical injury unit at the hospital. He's got more wires and tubes coming out of him than you could shake a stick at. He was found lying in a pool of puke and piss ten minutes from home. Somebody had taken a baseball bat to him. Battered him to a pulp – fractured skull in two places, fractures to both arms, one broken patella and one displaced patella, broken eye socket, cheekbone. In short, he is a mess.'

'Prognosis?' asked Jamieson.

'The doctors say he'll live, but he has a lot of rehabilitation to go through. May need to learn how to walk and talk again.' Replied Paige. 'Look, I know this is an individual who in his short life has managed to make enough enemies for a lifetime and that almost any could be responsible, but I thought you'd like to know just in case it fits in with what you're doing.'

'Absolutely', said Jamieson, 'thanks for the heads up. Keep in touch, Steve; we should have a beer sometime.'

For the remainder of the journey to work, Jamieson processed what he had been told. Was it just a coincidence that someone who had been questioned, albeit loosely, in the case his team were dealing with had been the victim of a vicious attack, or was there a link? And if so, who? A warning from Di Angelo? Unlikely. Jason James? Not his style, surely?

When he arrived at work, it was eight-fifteen. The obligatory cup of Giorgio's finest coffee stood waiting for him on his desk. Stone and Johnson were already there, heads down, reviewing what had been gleaned from the door-to-door enquiries and any CCTV and doorbell camera footage. In truth, neither amounted to much. Some grainy images that could have been anyone fleetingly passing.

'Morning, Gentlemen', said Jamieson. 'Thank you for the coffee, as always gratefully received, and how were your respective weekends?'

Stone shrugged. 'Yep' was his response.

Johnson was more forthcoming: 'Well', he said, 'we beat the Met second XV on Saturday afternoon and celebrated hard, as you would expect. Yesterday was a day of recovery.'

Johnson played for the Bedfordshire Police Rugby Union Side. Jamieson envied him. He, too, was a rugby player back in the day. Now his knees were shot. Sometimes after Lucy had dragged him down the gym, he struggled to get upstairs at home without gripping the bannister and making old man noises with every step.

'Did you score?' he asked Johnson.

Johnson looked suitably embarrassed: 'Winning try in the last minute', he said. 'The boys from the Met were not very happy. It was lovely.' He smiled.

Jamieson chuckled, and even Stone broke into a big grin, 'Well done,' said Jamieson, 'always nice when the Met gets rolled by their parochial cousins.'

'Where's Claire?' asked Jamieson.

'She's with Lisa Wooster, seeing if anything else has turned up from the crime scene that might help', replied Stone.

Jamieson thought he should wait for Evason to return before having the morning briefing. Jamieson was tempted to tell them about his Saturday evening and the phone call this morning but resisted. Always important to play by team rules so everyone feels included and the outcomes are better.

Evason came in about twenty minutes later. Jamieson asked her whether there was anything more to report. She shook her head: 'Nothing really, but tech is getting close with the phones. Somebody should be with us later today to outline what they have found out.'

Jamieson opened the briefing meeting and told them about his Saturday evening with Tony Di Angelo and Hes and the news he had received this morning from Steve Paige about Michael Macklin.

Evason and Stone recounted their meeting on Saturday with Holly and her Mother and how they both felt that an attempt had been made to shoehorn Michael Macklin's name into their subconscious. Evason followed that up with details of the call from Mrs Matthews on Sunday morning. 'It felt like the name was being offered up as a smokescreen. It just didn't feel right. I don't know, can't quite put my finger on it.........'

Jamieson nodded, not so much in agreement, but rather an acknowledgement that sometimes in police work, things just don't sit right;. However, there is no actual hard evidence of fact, it was more of a feeling – a good intuition for a police officer to have.

'Oh,' said Evason ', I did get a call from the handler who took the emergency call from Holly on Tuesday night. Said it was probably Nothing, but there was something about the call that she wasn't happy about; she just wanted to run it past one of us. It's probably nothing, but I've arranged to meet her tomorrow when she comes off the night shift. Just the need for thoroughness, really.'

'Absolutely', agreed Jamieson. 'So, my overall feeling is that none of this is gang-related, however.....' There was a knock at the door. Jamieson looked up. 'Come in', he called.

The door opened, and it was Graham Mitchell from the tech team.

'Sorry to disturb' he said: 'Not much to report on the phones found on the victim. The burner had a lot of addresses on deleted text messages where presumably drop-offs were being made. You're welcome to have that information, but it would probably be more useful to the drugs team.' That was what Hess had told them when they had met with him. The addresses would all belong to small-time users, the majority of whom would already be known to the police, so no real breakthrough there.

'However,' continued Mitchell. With a sense of drama, he held up an evidence bag; the corner pinched between his thumb and index finger. It contained a bashed-up mobile phone. The screen was smashed and fractured. Mitchell continued 'this was found yesterday by two paramedics doing their weekly ambulance clean. It had been pushed into a small space where it couldn't be easily found. They checked the manifest for all jobs over the last week.' He paused, possibly for further dramatic effect: 'On Tuesday evening, it was the ambulance that took Holly Matthews to the hospital.'

He let that sink in. Jamieson looked at Evason. Evason looked at Stone. Johnson looked at them all - he could barely contain himself.

Mitchell continued: 'it's pretty beaten up, but we have established a few initial things you ought to know.' He pushed the index finger of his left hand back using the fingers of his right hand: 'One - it appears to be Holly Matthews' phone; the number corresponds with her provider, so we're are fairly certain of that.' The middle finger next. 'Two - although there is some tracking software downloaded on there, it doesn't correspond with what we know was Ashley's phone number, so it seems unlikely that she was tracking him unless he had another phone we haven't found. We haven't been able to establish who the tracked number is registered to. We did call the number, but the phone is switched off........'

Another pause.

'And three?' Said, Jamieson.

Ring finger paused back: 'Three', said Mitchell. 'It appears that thirty seconds before she called emergency services, she called another number.'

Significant factors two and three right on cue.

Chapter Twenty-Seven

Monday 16th November – 10:45

'Why wouldn't she just remove the SIM card?' Asked Johnson. 'It would have made it much more difficult for us to trace.'

Stone answered: 'Imagine the stress she was under. She'd just seen her son driven away in an ambulance, possibly having seen him alive for the last time. Something that we need to get to the bottom of was happening. She was trying to process all of this and hide something away whilst under the gaze of the ambulance staff. Stress makes you do strange things and take chances you normally wouldn't. She probably thought trying to smash the thing was her best option at the time. She must've known it would be found sooner or later.'

Mitchell had taken his leave. Although he had taken the phone with him for further investigation, he had scribbled down the number that Holly Matthews had called just before reporting her son's stabbing to the emergency services.

Mitchell said they were trying to establish who the phone was registered to. It was against police procedure to call the number as it could be detrimental to the case moving forwards. He should know who it was registered to by this time tomorrow and will let Jamieson know as soon as he did.

The team regrouped - it had been one hell of a morning.

'What now?' Asked Stone.

'Well', said Jamieson ', we clearly need to be speaking to Holly Matthews again. This time, preferably, without her overbearing mother with her.'

'Good luck with that.' Stone contributed. 'She's horrendous.' He shivered at the thought.

'Do you think that Holly stabbed her own son?' asked Evason. 'I ask, but I have no idea why she would do that. And who is the mystery person she is speaking to while Ashley is lying in her arms dying?'

Jamieson rubbed his fingers across the bottom half of his face. It occurred to him that although he had shaved this morning, he hadn't done so very well. There were patches of stubble that he had missed.

He picked up the piece of paper that Mitchell had left with the phone number scribbled. He knew they all knew that if they knew the phone's owner to which this number belonged, they would have another piece of the jigsaw.

Jamieson rubbed his face again. It annoyed him. He was usually well turned out, if a little tired round the edges, and his clumsy attempts at this morning's shave made him think that everyone was looking at him.

'Sod it', he said, pressing the hands-free button on the phone directly before him. Then, he dialled the number from the paper. Every time he pushed a digit, an accusatory beep reminded him that he was acting against standard police procedure, 'you really should wait,' it seemed to be saying to him.

Finally, the call connected.

One ring.

Two rings.

A voice: 'Hello, you've reached the voicemail service of Davey Mcniven. I'm sorry I can't take your call. Please leave a message, and I will get back to you as soon as I can.'

Jamieson hung up.

Chapter Twenty-Eight

Monday 16th November – 15:00

Davey Mcniven had been safely installed in interview room one and Holly Matthews in interview room five - Jamieson liked the symmetry. The station had five interview rooms, and these two were at either end of the corridor, a bit like bookends. Maybe, thought Jamieson, these two are the bookends of this case. Then again, perhaps he had been reading too many detective stories.

They had been bought in within five minutes of each other on Jamieson's express instructions. He had told the Duty Sergeant responsible for booking suspects in that he had to 'damn well make sure that they saw each other in custody' and the Duty Sergeant, steeped in experience, 'damn well' made sure they had.

As Mcniven was waiting to be moved to a holding cell, Holly was led in for processing.

Holly gave Mcniven a cursory glance, then lowered her eyes with a seeming lack of indifference to the situation or, indeed, person. Mcniven became agitated as if trying to get a secret message across to Holly even though there were half a dozen police officers in the vicinity.

While the processing of Holly continued, Mcniven was moved to a holding cell to await an interview. Holly followed soon after to her holding cell.

That was three hours ago. Jamieson did not necessarily subscribe to the 'make them sweat' school of policing. There were genuine reasons why the interviews could not proceed straight away. However, he did acknowledge that a couple or three hours' wait would work in his favour, particularly with Davey Mcniven, who paced the holding cell, jumping at the slightest sound. The man was on edge.

The mystery call made by Holly to Mcniven needed answering, so both parties were bought in.

Locating Mcniven was a simple task. As Jamieson had suspected, he was at the football club. The officers sent to bring him in said he was compliant and, weirdly, almost waiting for them to turn up. He did not need cuffing and sat quietly in the back of the car for the journey.

Bringing Holly in was perceived to be more problematic.

They knew where she would be - that was not the problem.

They also knew that Mrs Matthews would be there - that was the problem.

Jamieson sent Evason and Johnson with the officers charged with picking Holly up. It was problematic but not that problematic.

The two young daughters were there when they arrived and, despite her apparent hatred of everything and everyone, when it came to the girls, Mrs Matthews would not go hard in their presence.

As it was, the officers were not needed. Holly travelled to the station in the unmarked car with Evason and Johnson.

On the one occasion Mrs Matthews threatened to cut loose, Holly calmly said: 'Not in front of the girls, please, Mum.' And any impending explosion was defused.

'How long will you have her?' asked Mrs Matthews.

'Depends how quickly she answers our questions.' replied Evason, without any irony.

Holly kissed the girls and told them Nanny would look after them this evening. They may even get a Mcdonald's if they behave.

As they left, Evason turned to Mrs Matthews: 'We will keep you posted; it must be difficult for you.'

'Thank you', she replied, almost gratefully but not quite.

On arrival at the police station, both parties were offered, lawyers. Mcniven declined; Holly said, 'Yes, please.'

So, a duty lawyer was contacted to sit in on Holly's interview. She had turned up about an hour ago and had gone straight in to talk to her client.

Jamieson divvied up the interview teams. Having previously met him, he and Stone would take Mcniven, and Evason and Johnson, with Evason leading, would take Holly.

The duty solicitor was Anna Chaston. She came with a fierce reputation, but Jamieson had always found her fair to deal with. She was upfront but told you how it was. There was no hidden agenda.

Evason liked Anna Chaston.

Early in her career with the Bedfordshire constabulary, Evason had been involved in a case where Chaston was representing the defendant, a sleazy individual charged with knocking his wife about. Chaston got him off.

After, when the prosecution team were licking their wounds in the local bar, Chaston came in with her team, minus the defendant. After a couple of hours of drinking and thinning of numbers, Evason, emboldened as usual by alcohol, approached Chaston intending to give her a piece of her mind.

'Your client not celebrating then?' she asked.

Chaston looked at her: 'Christ no, the man's a scumbag.'

'But it didn't stop you defending him?' said Evason, immediately wishing she had not.

Chaston looked at her quizzically but not unkindly: 'It's Claire, isn't it?'

Evason nodded: 'Well, Claire, that's my job. I don't have to like the people I defend; I have to ensure they get the best defence available to them. I'm guessing you don't like every 'victim' you get to deal with? Well, the same thing applies to me.' She tilted her head towards Evason conspiratorially, and Evason leant in. Chaston continued: 'Between you and me, whilst your efforts were exemplary, some of your colleagues' efforts came up well short. Your client had taken up with another bloke with a similar track record to her husband, who liked using his fists rather than talking. He needed to be thoroughly investigated and discounted before this came to court. Lazy police work made my job much easier........' she shrugged '.....I'll bet that somewhere down the line, my 'client' will get his comeuppance, just not today.'

They spent the rest of the evening together, drinking Pinot Grigio long after everyone else had drifted off. When Jamieson heard, he laughed. He wondered how many blokes had tried their luck at chatting up those two only to be sent spinning away back to their mates with a caustic comment ringing in their ears and their cheeks burning.

Anna Chaston came out of the interview room and walked over to Evason smiling: 'Hello Claire,' she said, 'I'm afraid I'm advising a 'no comment' interview with this one.' Then, she pulled a pained face: 'Sorry.'

Evason smiled back: 'I expected nothing else, to be honest. We will be starting in a minute. Is everything else in order? Does your client need a comfort break? Fresh water?'

'I think she's fine, but I will ask.' She headed back to interview room five.

Jamieson, Stone and Johnson joined Evason: 'Okay,' said Jamieson ', Let's do this. Good luck, everybody.' And they headed off in their pairings, hoping to get some answers.

Chapter Twenty-Nine

Monday 16th November – 15:10

Interview room one

'So, Davey,' began Jamieson. 'When we last spoke and asked you about the night of 11th November, to be clear, the night that Ashley James died, you told us that you were down at the football club, and someone came in about half past eight or thereabouts and said that he'd heard from his girlfriend that Ashley was dead. After that, you were due to go on a night shift, but by the time you got home, you didn't think you could face work, so you called in sick and fell asleep in the kitchen. You felt better when you woke up around two, so you went to work for the remainder of your shift, which finished at seven.'

Jamieson looked up from his notes: 'Is that about right?' he asked.

Mcniven licked his lips and nodded: 'That sounds about right. I mean, from what I can remember,' he answered.

Jamieson sat back and cleared his throat: 'It was a Champions League night that night, and the game was being shown on the club's wide-screen TV. So, lots of people were in, and most of them confirm that chain of events.......'

Mcniven nodded.

'.....but none recall seeing or talking to you when the news broke. There's just no recollection by anyone of you being there.'

'Well', said Mcniven ', It doesn't mean I wasn't, does it? I was working behind the bar for most of the night, and people were facing the tv in the opposite direction. They may just not have noticed me, surely?' He shrugged.

Jamieson nodded: 'No, no, you're right. But it would have been helpful if someone had though. You can see how that might be, can't you, Davey?'

Mcniven nodded. Shrugged again: 'I suppose.' He said.

Jamieson continued: 'Do you remember who else was working behind the bar that night?'

Mcniven nodded again: 'Yes, that was Debbie and Sean.'

This time Jamieson nodded: 'Now Sean says that these nights are a bit manic. Up to a hundred people could watch the game and require constant service. He recalls it being busy and can't remember seeing you there, but he said he was so run off his feet, he can't be entirely sure.......'

Mcniven waited.

'....... but Debbie is a bit different.'

Jamieson paused. Mcniven shifted slightly in his seat.

'Now Debbie recalls you getting a call just before kick-off, kick off that night was seven forty-five, and she knows it was your phone because your ring tone is the theme to Match of the Day.'

'Ah well', said Mcniven, a degree of relief creeping onto his face, 'A few of the lads at the club have got that as a ringtone. It could have been any of them.'

'She also saw you answer it and speak to someone,' added Jamieson. 'Plus, she saw you put your coat on and go out the back door to the car park.'

Mcniven shrugged: 'Perhaps a barrel needed changing, I really can't remember, sorry.'

Jamieson placed his elbows on the table and bought the palms of his hands together in a praying position. 'Now you've surrendered your phone to us, but you've wiped any recent activity - calls, texts, messages - all gone. Now that technology is what it is, we can recover all this information, but it will take some time.'

He looked straight into Mcniven's eyes.

'So, Davey,' he said, 'tell me who the call was from and what it was about?'

Interview room five

Evason began: 'Holly, I'm going to go back over the events of 11th November. Now I fully appreciate that this was a traumatic night for you, and I don't want to upset you in any way. So, if you start feeling stressed, please make me or your solicitor aware, and we can take a break. Yes?'

Holly nodded.

'Now, that evening, you told us you were using tracking software to follow Ashley. You had concerns because Ashley had come into some big sums of cash, and you didn't know where from. Is that correct so far?'

Holly scratched her head: 'No comment,' she replied.

'Ok. Now around twenty-to-eight, you came up Holmes Road, where it joins with Rankin Avenue, and you found

Ashley lying on the ground with a wound to his leg and a significant amount of blood still coming out of the wound. Is that correct?'

'No comment.'

'So, you've told us that no one else was around, and you called the emergency services immediately. You didn't call anyone else first?'

Holly yawned: 'No comment.' She said again.

'Ok', persevered Evason. 'So you were on the phone with the emergency services for just short of four minutes. The call handler talked you through applying a tourniquet to the wound, and the ambulance arrived. Is that right?'

'I suppose so', said Holly. Anna Chaston put her hand on Holly's forearm. Holly sighed: 'I mean, NO COMMENT.'

'Now, sometime between your calling the emergency services and arriving at the hospital, you mislaid your phone, is that correct?'

'Yes.' Again Anna Chaston touched Holly's forearm. 'What?' snapped Holly. 'I did; I'm not telling them anything they don't already know.'

Evason noted a wrinkle of concern on Anna Chaston's normally crease-free brow - her client was getting slightly rattled.

Evason shuffled through her notes and found a photo of the smashed phone. 'Now.' She put the picture on the desk in front of Holly. 'This was found in the ambulance you travelled to the hospital that night. Is it yours?'

'For fuck's sake.' Said Holly, spreading her hands in front of her in apparent frustration: 'It's an iPhone. They must sell about thirty million each year. Yes, it might be mine. No, it's not mine. What do you want me to say?'

This time Anna Chaston leant forward and whispered in Holly's ear. Holly nodded, angled her head and lifted her hand across her mouth to whisper to Chaston without being heard.

Chaston nodded, then said, 'We'd like a break in the next five minutes, please.'

Evason nodded: 'Of course. Just a couple more questions for now.'

'The data retrieved so far from this phone.' She pointed at the photo. 'Indicates that a call was made to Emergency Services at seven forty..........'

'Which is exactly what I did.' Snapped Holly

'So, you are saying that it is your phone?' Asked Evason, her brow furrowed extravagantly in mock confusion.

Holly realised her error: 'No comment.' Chaston looked frustrated.

'........however, at seven thirty-nine, the phone was used to call a number that belongs to Davey Mcniven.' Evason narrowed her eyes for the coup de grace. "I just wondered why, with your son bleeding to death in front of your eyes, you would call Davey Mcniven?'

'Interview suspended', said Evason, snapping off the recording device before either Holly or Anna Chaston could get the 'No' of 'No comment' out.

Chapter Thirty

Monday 16th November – 16:40

Jamieson's mobile rang.

He looked at the screen. It was the Chief Constable Peter Jarman.

Jamieson answered and moved away from the general throng of the operations room.

'Sir,' he said.

'Alex,' said Jarman. 'What's the state of play?'

Jamieson outlined where the investigation currently stood.

"What next, then?' asked Jarman.

'Just debating on whether to retain them overnight, sir. Make them sweat a bit, try again in the morning,' replied Jamieson.

'Bit of a political hot potato, this one, Alex.' Yes, thought Jamieson, so you keep saying. A young black victim of knife crime, I get it.

'I think you need more, Alex, if you're going to keep them in; imagine the uproar if the mother is not involved and the police were holding her overnight whilst she was still grieving for her dead son. The press would have a field day with the force.'

'With respect, sir, she is involved. She won't tell us to what extent.' Said, Jamieson. He didn't play politics particularly well. He tried to react to the situation as it played out before him – not much time for niceties. He rarely questioned authority, but his frustration was starting to surface.

'Let them go, Alex.' Said, Jarman. 'Build a stronger case, and you can bring them back in with a greater chance of getting a result. Unless, of course, you think there's a chance of them absconding?'

'No, sir. I don't see that. The mother has daughters at home, and, as for Mcniven, I don't think he's got it in him.'

'I can hear in your voice, Alex, that you disagree with me on this one. You'll have to trust me. If it goes wrong, I'll take it on the chin. I hope you know that is the case.'

Jamieson did know that. Jarman was the ultimate politician, but he did not hang his officers out to dry; as long as they stuck to the rules, regulations, and various protocols, he would always back them up.

And, as always, Jarman was gone without a 'goodbye', leaving Jamieson listening to a deadline.

Jamieson went back to the others.

'Listen up,' he said, raising his hands to get their attention. 'We're letting them go for this evening.'

Stone began to object; Jamieson held his hand up to stop him: 'Orders from above, I'm afraid. I'm not saying I agree with or disagree with them, just that I must follow them.'

Stone muttered under his breath. It sounded like 'bloody politics.'

'Rog,' said Jamieson ', Can you get the desk sergeant to start the process of getting them released. Best arrange for a couple of squad cars to take them home, might as well go the whole hog.

'Tuck them up in bed as well.' Said Stone. And before Jamieson could tell him to shut up, he grinned as if to say, 'I know, I know!' Hands raised in mock surrender.

Jamieson checked his watch: five-thirty.

'Ok.' He said, 'that's been a long day, and we've made some headway but not enough. Go home, go to the gym, listen to some music, relax – see if any more ideas come to you, any avenues we haven't considered. We'll reconvene in the morning. Claire, see you after your meeting, hope it goes well.'

On the drive home, Jamieson called Billy Watson.

'How are ticket sales going?' he asked.

'Pretty good last time I spoke to the pub landlord', replied Watson. 'Well over a hundred, and there's still a couple of weeks to go.'

'Got the setlist sorted out?' enquired Jamieson.

'Ninety per cent there,' said Watson. 'Going for a big ending to this one. Send the crowd home happy in time for Christmas.'

They talked a bit more. Billy told Jamieson how much he missed his Mum, who had died earlier in the year. He was the only one from his family left now. He had no brothers or sisters, and his Dad had gone many years back. Jamieson thought about Billy's life – no significant other half, and to Jamieson's recollection, there never had been. Many attractive women had adorned Billy's arm over the years but never for very long. They would disappear to be replaced by another similar-looking woman – Billy certainly had his type – and the cycle continued. As the years passed, Billy looked a bit older, but funnily the women never did.

Jamieson got home. Lucy passed him at the front door.

'I'm off to a Zumba class.' She said, pecking at his cheek. 'There's pasta with a sauce keeping warm in the oven. 'Pasta', thought Jamieson. 'Great!'

He went upstairs and changed from his work attire – suit on the hanger with his tie, shirt and socks in the laundry basket - into his evening wear, track bottoms and t-shirt.

He went downstairs into the living room and picked up the tv remote, thought better of it, and teed up some music on the iPad – Cowboy Junkies, one of his favourites, but not Lucy's, so he often took the opportunity of listening to them while she was not around.

He got his dinner from the oven and sat on the sofa to eat it.

While he did, he googled 'knife crime statistics uk' on the iPad.

It didn't make for enjoyable reading. Knife crime was second only to reports of sexual offences over the past few years. Both very distasteful, and both on the increase – a worrying trend.

The piece he read gave some statistics which showed that the most significant increase in victims of knife crime was in young men aged between sixteen and twenty-five. It seemed rarely did it affect females. The perpetrators of knife crime were, unsurprisingly, from the same age group and, again, mainly male.

The piece discussed the influence of violent and graphic computer games and other media, television, film and music. This interested Jamieson greatly. He could see how visual images could affect a young person but had never considered that music, or, more to the point, lyrics from songs, could change how a person thought, how a person processed life and their surroundings, but he supposed that it did. Perhaps some of these millionaire musicians needed to start taking responsibility for the message they were giving the young people who hung on to their every word.

The influence of America was also put forward as being critical. The writer drew a comparison with gun crime in the States – after all, the second amendment spoke of the right to keep and bear arms – well, that wasn't just guns. A knife was still an 'arm', surely? Difficult to argue that it wasn't.

The main reason that young men convicted of knife crimes put forward were the need for self-defence. 'It was either him or me', 'I went out with a knife to prevent anything happening', and 'I was scared to leave home without something I could use to defend myself'.

Jamieson thought about his investigation. As far as they were aware, Ashley James was unarmed. So, he probably didn't meet the expected profile of a knife victim in the UK. From Jamieson's discussion with Tony Di Angelo, Ashley seemed as far removed from what an expected victim would be as possible. Ashley was bright and focused and would surely have sensed danger, and if he felt too exposed, he would have fled. He was an athlete; he could have outrun any potential assailant. And yet he let his killer get close enough to plunge a blade into his leg.

Perhaps, Jamieson thought, it was someone he trusted, someone he knew.

Chapter Thirty-One

Monday 16th November – 17:35

Stone was like a man on a mission.

Usually, in these circumstances, he would have been in Jamieson's ear: 'Come on, Alex, keep them in overnight. They both know something, and they're not talking – let's sweat it out of them.' But aside from a few barbed comments, he had left well alone.

Because tonight was different, tonight, for the first time in over thirty years, Stone had a date.

He was almost relieved when the Chief Constable decided that it was in the best interests of the investigation to let Holly and Mcniven go home. It meant that, for once, Stone could get an early evening in.

As Stone made his way out, Johnson called after him: 'Sandy, fancy a quick pint on the way home?' And Stone had to turn him down. That was a shame because he had grown fond of the younger man and enjoyed spending time with him. He almost felt like a father figure. Stone had no sons or daughters – it had just never happened for him and Margaret.

Earlier in the hectic day, at twelve-thirty, Stone had announced that he was on a coffee run. Orders were called out, and everyone always had the same thing, so there was no need to write anything down, and Stone set off to Giorgio's.

Halfway there, he stopped and stepped into the entrance of a shop that had closed down some time ago. He pulled his phone out and found the number he was looking for. He paused and went through the conversation in his head. He had been rehearsing it for the last couple of days and had it just about off-pat.

He figured that at twelve-thirty, teachers, including acting head teachers, would be either in the staff room or sat at a desk in their classroom while the students were either in the school canteen or, in the case of the older ones, down at the local fast food restaurants.

He poked at the call button, took a deep breath and waited.

'Helen Miller.'

Stone's pre-planned script went out of the window. He became a spluttering fool: 'Er, hi, it, um, Sandy. Sandy Stone. Pete.'

'Sorry, who?' Asked Helen.

'Policeman. Pete Stone. Saturday. You phoned.' It came across as a string of random words, but it made sense.

'Oh, DS Stone.' Stone breathed a sigh of relief: she knew who he was. 'How lovely to hear from you. After my disastrous effort on Saturday morning, I wondered whether I might have managed to scare you off.'

'Takes more than that to put me off,' said Stone with a chuckle.

They passed a few more minutes together before Stone plucked up the courage to say: 'Anyway, you mentioned something about meeting for a drink..........?'

'Yes, yes,' said Helen hoping not to sound overly keen, desperate even, and failing miserably.

'Well,' said Stone ', I would like that very much. When do you........?'

'I'm free tonight,' blurted Helen. Dammit, woman, calm down. 'I mean if you're around.'

Stone, acting very gentlemanly, merely said: 'Absolutely. Dinner, perhaps?'

So, it was all agreed. Helen knew a lovely gastro pub and would phone and book for eight. They would meet there as it was midway between where they each lived.

Stone drove home with a mixture of anticipation and dread. He was aware of the adrenaline pumping around his body.

He felt like a sixteen-year-old going on a first date.

He arrived home at six thirty. Home was currently a rented one-bed flat into which he had moved when Margaret had returned home. Given the circumstances, neither felt it was proper for them to live under the same roof. Stone believed that if they were no longer man and wife, it would be wrong to live like man and wife. Stone arriving home to his dinner on the table or Saturday morning at the supermarket had a hollow ring to it.

Stone laid out what he would wear on the bed and jumped in the shower. He dried off, shaved for the second time that day, and put on some deodorant and aftershave

– he hadn't worn aftershave for a few years now – cleaned his teeth and got dressed into a polo shirt and chinos with a blue linen jacket (that Margaret had bought him) and his smart brown brogues. The chinos and the jacket were noticeably snugger than the last time he had worn them.

The journey to the pub was only eight miles, around fifteen minutes at this time of the evening. Stone checked his watch: seven o'clock. In his excitement, he was ready too soon and had a forty-minute wait until it was time to leave. He didn't want to be early. That would be far too keen.

He sat down and turned the television on. Watched for about five minutes, then turned it off again. He rechecked his watch: five past seven this time.

Then he remembered road works around where he was going or did he? Had he just made that up?

At ten past seven, he left the house. He remembered that there were roadworks in that area.

At seven twenty-five, he pulled into the pub car park. There were no roadworks.

He sat in his car for twenty minutes. Other people going into the restaurant looked in his car as they passed. So who was this strange man, sitting in his car in a dark pub car park?

At ten to eight, he entered the restaurant and waited in the foyer. Suddenly he could not remember what Helen looked like. Was she tall or short? Did she have dark hair? Or light hair? Was she wearing glasses? He was starting to panic.

'Hello, Peter.' Stone looked up. Shortish, dark hair, no glasses. Helen leaned in and gave him a peck on the cheek.

Stone stepped back: 'You look lovely,' he said, smiling and gesturing towards the restaurant entrance. 'Shall we?'

As it was, Stone did not need a pick to break the ice. The conversation flowed, and Helen was terrific company. She thanked him again for addressing the school, and again, he modestly said that it was nothing. They talked about her asking him for a drink, with Claire Evason listening in: 'That was so embarrassing.' She said: 'I'm even going red now thinking about it.' They laughed about it. 'Claire is as good as gold.' Said Stone. 'It is exactly the sort of thing that she would do herself.'

They talked about their jobs – Helen had been a teacher all her working life and had only just made the leap to acting head teacher. She still wasn't sure it was the right thing for her. She felt she was too long in the tooth to learn new skills – they talked about holidays, favourite television programmes, favourite songs, and books.

Funnily, Margaret was also a teacher. So what was it about him and the teaching profession, Stone wondered?

The conversation was effortless, and the more it went on, the more Stone could feel himself relax.

They ordered: Helen had calamari and crab linguine; Stone, ever the traditionalist, went for a prawn cocktail followed by a steak and chips. Helen teased him gently: 'And a black forest gateau for dessert?' She asked. 'Very retro.' She approved.

They were both driving, so they limited themselves to one small glass of wine. That wasn't an issue for Stone. For once, he didn't need to overdose on too much alcohol to get through the evening.

As the waiter cleared away the plates for the main course, Stone excused himself.

He finished his business and washed and dried his hands. As he left the restroom, he took out his mobile phone to see if he had any messages; looking down, he failed to notice the door of the ladies opening and a woman stepping out into the corridor. Stone almost, but not quite, crashed into her.

'Oh, my God.' He said, 'I am so sorry.'

He looked up into the woman's face. It was the face that he had known for over thirty years. It was a face he knew inside out.

'Margaret.' He said, his mouth hanging open with surprise.

'Pete.' She replied, looking a bit uncomfortable. 'What are you doing here?'

'Um.' Began Stone. 'Um, a bit awkward actually; I'm, um, on a first date with someone.'

Margaret had a face like thunder; then she broke into a wide smile: 'So am I,' she giggled. 'Isn't it awful? I've had to have four glasses of wine to keep it interesting. He must think I'm an alcoholic!' She touched his shoulder as she spoke.

Stone wanted to say: 'No, actually, I'm having a really nice time.' But knew better.

Instead, he said: 'Look, I must go back. I'll give you a call later in the week.'

Margaret smiled and said: 'Have a great time. Hope you get lucky!'

'Jesus.' thought Stone, returning to the table: 'Of all the bloody evenings!'

Dessert had arrived, and although the evening never quite reached the heights of Stone's pre-Margaret encounter, Stone instinctively felt comfortable with Helen. He had a nervous moment over coffee when he asked whether she would like to meet up at the weekend and initially thought he had misread the signs. Helen took out her phone and scrolled down her diary: 'When were you thinking?' She asked. 'I've got a few bits and pieces booked, but I'd bump any of them to spend more time with you.'

They split the bill. Stone began to protest, but Helen soon shut him down: 'If you want to spend time with me,' she said, 'then you will let me pay my way.'

Stone helped her with her coat and walked her to her car. Helen leant in again and, this time, kissed him gently on the mouth. 'See you Saturday,' she said, getting into her car, 'text me the details of where and when.'

Stone drove home in seventh heaven. He had a permanent grin, and even the love songs on the radio, which usually annoyed him, sounded that much sweeter tonight.

He got home and realised that his earlier adrenaline hadn't entirely dissipated. He wasn't tired and would not get off to sleep. He put his phone on charge and went into the bedroom to change. His belly sprung out a bit when he unbuttoned his trousers (must get back to the gym, he thought), and he used hangers for his chinos, polo shirt and jacket. His socks, clean on this evening, would do for work tomorrow. He slung on his track bottoms and a t-shirt.

He went into the front room and switched on the television. There was a documentary series he had been watching, and one might bring on a bit of weariness, enough to send him off to sleep anyway.

Twenty minutes in, and he had drifted off. Suddenly he sat bolt upright. Off in the distance, he could hear his phone ringing. Now, where the bloody hell had he left it? This would be work and no doubt something important.

He found it where he had left it, charging in the kitchen. He grabbed it and pulled out the charging lead in one motion, didn't bother to check the name on the screen, so convinced was he that it would work.

'Stone', he said, somewhat breathlessly.

'Pete,' said, to him, an instantly recognisable voice, even slurred with alcohol. It was Margaret. 'Oh, Pete, are we making a big mistake here?' She was crying.

'Oh,' thought Stone, 'shit!'

Chapter Thirty-Two

Monday 17th November – 17:40

Evason gathered up her belongings and pushed them into her bag. She checked her watch: five forty-five. Now that Holly and Mcniven had been allowed to go home, there wasn't much more that could be achieved tonight, but she could do a bit of team building.

When Johnson's offer of a quick one after work had been declined by Stone, as he left hurriedly, Johnson looked a bit taken aback. That had never happened before; Stone was always around after work for a drink or two. Even Jamieson sitting at his desk, raised an eyebrow when Johnson's offer was turned down. He caught Evason's eye and made a face as if to say, 'what's that all about?'

As Evason passed Johnson's desk, she stopped: 'I don't drink pints, and I don't know much about rugby, but I could kill for a glass of something; it's been a long day.'

'Ah!' Said Johnson, packing away his desk and reaching for his coat. 'A sympathy beer. Never let it be said that having a sympathy beer is beneath me.' He grinned, reached for the door and swept an open arm towards the exit: 'after you.' Although Evason was not one for old school, 'ladies first' niceties, she smiled.

The Duke was just across the road from the station and was an old-fashioned kind of pub. The bar was 'L' shaped, and the seating booths wrapped themselves around. There were some real ales and the more standard, recognisable beers. There was an extensive range of gins but not so much in the way of white wines. Evason mulled it over. She reckoned she could have one gin and tonic and a soft drink or two small glasses of white wine, assuming they would stay for two drinks, which they would.

'Gin and tonic, please.' She answered when Johnson asked: 'Bombay Sapphire and Fever Tree, ice and lemon' just a single, please.' She found a booth, took her coat off and slid in. Johnson followed soon after. He put the drinks on the table and moved Evason's glass and a bottle of tonic water across to her. He waited for her to pour the tonic into the gin before he tilted his glass towards her: 'Cheers.' He said. She clinked and responded with her own 'cheers'.

They discussed Stone and how it was not like him to turn a beer down and debated what he might be up to.

'Well,' said Johnson ', whatever it is, good luck to him; he looked very pleased with himself, didn't he?'

Evason wondered whether it might have anything to do with the call that she had been inadvertently part of on Saturday but chose not to mention it to Johnson. After all, everyone deserves a bit of happiness - and privacy.

They discussed the case. Evason mentioned that she was due with the Emergency Response Centre first thing in the morning. She didn't expect anything to come of it, probably just the handler being a bit paranoid, looking for some af-firmation that she did everything right and followed the correct processes and protocols. That was fine, Evason knew that was a tough job, and if ten minutes of her time could make someone feel better about themselves, then it was time well spent.

Johnson mentioned that he had been speaking with Lisa Wooster. Nothing else had come to light, although the area was still being cordoned off and policed twen-ty-four hours a day. There had been an outpouring of emotion around what had happened, particularly about the victim. It seems that Ashley James was a well-loved individual, and people were still trying to process his death and, possibly, his involvement with a gang. It just wasn't his style.

'Apparently, there are thousands of flowers, teddies, balloons, and handwritten notes. Lisa says she's never seen anything like it in all her time with the force. Not quite Princess Di but certainly Bedfordshire's equivalent.'

He continued: 'She did say that Holly Matthews had been there on several occasions, just standing and crying for hours.'

Although Evason wasn't a mother, her recent change of heart gave her a better perspective of Holly's situation.

'She's a mother, I guess; goes with the territory' was all she offered.

'No sign of Mrs Matthews, Holly's mum, I mean.' Said, Johnson.

Evason shrugged: 'No real surprise there either.'

They entered a moment of silence, not awkward by any standards, two people contemplating a situation.

The Johnson spoke: 'What did you make of the Chief's Constable's decision to let them go home for the night? Shouldn't we have made them sweat it out and see what happened?'

Evason wrinkled her nose: 'Tricky,' she answered. 'After all, Holly is a grieving mother, and that needs to be considered. And if you are letting her go, then you probably have to let Mcniven go as well. I think that Holly knows more, but of the two, Mcniven is the weaker character and more likely to crack. Also, Holly is impetuous and may give something away in anger, but she does have her brief with her, policing her answers.'

'How well do you know the Chief Constable?' enquired Johnson. 'I mean, he comes across as a decent bloke, right?'

For a moment, Evason wondered what Johnson had heard. Were there rumours on the grapevine? They had been so careful; surely there couldn't be. She looked at Johnson. He was staring intently at her, waiting for an answer. She decided that he had innocently stumbled into her private life.

She answered: 'He's charismatic, that's for sure. But put him in charge of a case like this one, and he'd be lost. Much better someone like Alex, far more methodical, but put him in a roomful of journalists, politicians and angry members of the public, and he'd hold his own, and most of them would buy into what he was telling them. He would make a great politician. Wouldn't surprise me if he went into public office when he retired.' She was being a bit naughty now. Jarman had mentioned public office as an option for when he left the force.

Evason bought a second round of drinks—another pint for Johnson and an orange juice for herself.

They sat and talked for a further half an hour.

Evason debated telling Johnson about her illicit affair, not who it was with, but about all the sneaking about, the guarded phone conversations. Apart from Jarman himself, she had shared this private information with no one else. She had a strong relationship with her mother, but not the type of relationship where, well, relationships were discussed. Her mother was old-fashioned. Marriage was a sanctity not to be taken lightly.

She liked Johnson, and it would have been good to talk to someone else to get a different view on what she was doing, but she decided not tonight, maybe in the future.

Ironically, Johnson was thinking the same thing about his private life. He liked Evason. She took things at face value and would not rush to judge.

Sometimes Johnson annoyed himself. He liked to tell himself that his private life was precisely that -private. But really, was he hiding his true identity? He wasn't himself entirely, that was for sure.

He realised he didn't want to be judged, judged by society, judged by his peers. Who did? Being judged was against most people's instincts.

Evason would be an excellent person to talk to to get a different viewpoint, but he decided not tonight but definitely in the future.

At seven-thirty, they got up to leave. When they opened the door, the rain of the last week or so had upped itself a notch.

'Come on,' said Evason ', I'll drop you off home.'

'On this occasion, you will not get an argument from me', said Johnson looking up into the dark night sky. 'This is getting biblical.'

After five minutes in the car, Johnson said: 'That's great, just here, please, on the left. There's a vegetarian shop. I need to pick up some dinner for this evening.'

He jumped out. Evason lowered the window and leant across the passenger seat.

Johnson spoke first: 'Thanks, Claire, that was really good, just what I needed. Drive safely, and I'll see you in the morning.'

Evason smiled and gestured towards the vegetarian shop with a dip of her head, 'Enjoy your dinner. See you tomorrow.'

As she pulled away, she thought Johnson was a good colleague. She realised that she liked working where she did and that, in their own ways, they all added something to the collective. They are four very different characters but all with a common goal. She realised that she was sounding a bit cheesy now, so she made herself stop.

She glanced in the rear-view mirror and could make out the rain-soaked figure of Roger Johnson heading away from the vegetarian shop towards the very non-vegetarian kebab shop on the other side of the road.

She grinned.

Chapter Thirty-Three

Tuesday 17th November – 08:15

'It's like my Geoff always says,' said Mary, mashing a tea bag against the side of a mug, 'my job is about listening but also hearing. Geoff says that the reason I'm always talking at home is that I'm always listening at work.'

She took the milk from the fridge and cradled it whilst she thought about Geoff very fondly, thought Evason. 'He's on the vans is Geoff. A paramedic..' she explained. ....we both do shift work. They try to get our shifts in sync as far as possible, but sometimes we don't see much of each other for weeks on end. 'Ships in the night', says Geoff. We've been married forty-odd years.'

She unscrewed the lid of the milk. 'Was it milk and sugar, love?' She asked Evason.

'Just milk, please.' Came the reply.

Mary did the honours and stirred both mugs with a teaspoon. 'Help yourself to a biscuit.' She said, gesturing towards the tin with a tilt of her head, 'but steer clear of the custard creams. They're Jean's; she'll break your fingers if she sees you've had one.' She smiled.

Evason checked her watch - eight fifteen - Mary was on the back end of an eight-hour night shift but was as alert as many twenty-year-olds who have just had ten hours in bed. Mary eased herself into an armchair. 'We'll drink these, and then I'll take you into one of the offices. I hope I'm not wasting your time with this; it's just something doesn't quite sit right with it for me.'

'That's fine', said Evason. They were sitting in the staff room of the emergency call centre for Bedfordshire. 'How long have you been doing the job?' she asked.

'Oh, too long,' replied Mary, 'twenty-seven years or thereabouts.'

Evason had so much time for people who did jobs like Mary and Geoff. It was a vocation. She knew they were not very well rewarded for their critical role in society, yet the ones she had met were always cheerful and uncomplaining.

'You must enjoy it? I mean, to have stuck at it for so long.'

Mary considered: 'It has its moments, and there are some lovely people to work with here. But, you know, some of the things we have to deal with are very sad. After talking to that lad's Mother and finding out, he had died was very upsetting. I shed a few tears that night when I found out. That's part of it, I guess. When you hand over to the ambulance crew, you've done all you can and handed the situation over to the best people to deal with it. The problem is you rarely find out what the outcome is. Best not to dwell on it, really.'

'It's not all doom and gloom, though. There's one fellow phones up every night at three o'clock...' Mary leant forward, her voice dropped to a whisper '....he tells you what he's got in hand, what way he's got it pointed, how fast he's doing it, he even tells you what music he's listening to while he's doing it....I mean.....Jean says that last week he said he was listening to Whitney Houston, but in the background, she could hear the Royal Military Brass Band..he must have been going like the clappers to keep time to that..' she suddenly shrieked with laughter, 'with his own conductors' baton in his hand.'

Evason grinned and broke into laughter for the first time in what felt like ages.

''Ere,' said Mary. 'The girls all call him Mister Bates, and Jean says she hopes he hasn't got a son who'll take over from him, you know, Master........' she mimed the word 'Bates' and pulled a fake shocked face.

They talked and laughed for a further ten minutes whilst they finished off their tea. Then, finally, Mary stood and collected the mugs. She rinsed them and left them on the drainer.

'Well,' she said, 'let's do what you came here for. Follow me.'

Evason followed Mary down the corridor and into an office marked 'knock before entering'. Inside there was a desk with some sound equipment on it. They took a chair on each side of the desk facing each other.

Mary prepared the sound equipment but continued to talk while she did so.

'The manager here has a policy that when one of us is involved in a call that results in someone dying, we sit in here and do a debrief. I think it's a good thing. I don't think it's done as a 'well, you got this wrong, and you got that wrong'. It's more to reinforce what you've done, and if you could have done something different, what would you have done? That sort of thing.'

She continued to fiddle with the equipment: 'We can either listen to this through our own headphones or the speaker system. Any preference?'

'Let's go through the speaker system. We can always change to headphones if we need to.' Said Evason.

'Ok, I'll run the whole thing through first. It lasts for three minutes and forty-three seconds.'

She pressed the playback button, and the sound of the whole encounter filled the room through the speaker system. Evason closed her eyes, trying to get a better feeling for the events unfolding.

When the three minutes forty-three seconds was over, she sat back with two initial thoughts.

First, how desperate Holly Matthews sounded and how, when her judgement was not clouded by alcohol or drugs, she sounded so much clearer and how her ability to think was unburdened.

Secondly, she realised just how brilliant the sixty-plus-something jovial woman sitting before her was. She had complete control over the situation. She kept Holly calm and focused and delivered on her promise to get help there as soon as possible. Under four minutes to get an ambulance to the scene was, in Evason's opinion, a phenomenal piece of work all around.

'So that's it fully,' said Mary. 'Any thoughts?'

Evason muttered something about it being textbook which completely underplayed her admiration for Mary.

'My manager thought so too. And, without being big-headed about it, I felt it went as well as these things can, given the situation and outcome....'

'But.....' Mary let it hang for a moment: '....there was one thing I couldn't put my finger on, something about the call, it just didn't feel right. So, I asked my manager if I could listen through it a few more times, and she said as many times as I wanted. She's very good like that.'

Mary returned to the sound equipment and pressed more buttons: 'In the end, I nailed it down to this next extract. To be honest, two short words in this extract. Ready?'

She pressed play, and the noise of the call filled the room again:

'Curtain - Sunday - dial. I've sent those details to the attending crew. They will be with you as soon as they possibly can. What has happened?

Move. MOVE.

They will be with you as soon as possible. I need you to stay calm. Can you tell me what has happened?'

Mary stopped the playback.

'Anything?' She asked.

'Play it again, please.'

Mary played the same extract.

There was something there, Evason knew, but she couldn't put her finger on it.

Mary let her think for a few more minutes. Finally, she spoke: 'So this is where my old man Geoff is clever when he talks about listening and hearing because there is a difference.' She raised a finger: 'Can I tell you what I hear?'

Evason nodded.

'Two words.' Said, Mary. 'Actually, one word but repeated. The second time with more urgency than the first - MOVE.'

Evason was held enraptured.

'I think in that situation, most people would use an expression such as 'Get a move on' or, and she had already used an expletive earlier in the exchange, more likely to be, and please excuse my French, 'Get a fucking move on.' Or hurry or hurry up, please. It's just to me, in that conversation, in that exchange, the word 'move' on its own doesn't feel in the right context. I'm not a psychologist, and it is just a feeling, but, you know, I've been doing this for twenty-seven years, and I just know what feels right and what doesn't. And this doesn't!'

'Play it again, please, Mary', asked Evason.

Mary did.

'And once more, please.'

Mary was correct. It didn't feel right. The language, and the choice of word, was not correct.

'There is another thing,' said Mary

'Go on', said Evason.

Mary went back to the sound equipment. This time the extract she chose was slightly longer.

'Can you activate it and tell me the three words, please?

Ok, hold on, hold on. Ok, so curtain - Sunday - dial - please hurry.

Curtain - Sunday - dial. I've sent those details to the attending crew. They will be with you as soon as they possibly can. What has happened?

Move. MOVE.

They will be with you as soon as possible. I need you to stay calm. Can you tell me what has happened?

My son has been stabbed.'

Mary looked at Evason. 'I'll play it again, but this time listen to the volume of the bits the Mother says. Don't worry about my bits. Concentrate on the volume of what the Mother is saying.'

She played it again.

'What do you hear?' Asked Mary.

Evason thought: 'When she says 'move, move', it's quieter.' She said finally. 'You would think it would be louder because it's being said more urgently, but it's definitely quieter. Why?'

Mary sighed: 'Well, I have thought about that as well', she said, 'You must think I'm a regular Miss Marple.'

She patted her trouser pockets and pulled out her mobile phone. 'So, this is what I think.' She held the phone up to her ear with the microphone directly in front of her mouth. 'So, say I'm at home speaking to my friend Maureen. I hold the phone like this.'

'Then Geoff comes up and whispers ', do you want a cup of tea?' And when I answer him, so Maureen doesn't hear, I twist the phone away from my mouth. Like this.' She twisted the phone so that she could still hear what the person at the other end was saying but moved the mouthpiece away from her mouth so anything she said would not necessarily be heard. 'Yes, please, love and a biscuit.'

'That's what I think has happened here. Only the Mother hasn't turned the phone away sufficiently, and what she has said has still been picked up - 'move, move'. Mary spread her hands. 'Well, that's how it seems to me anyway.'

Evason looked at Mary. 'So, what you're saying is.....'

Mary finished: 'I'm saying that when Mum said 'move, move', she wasn't talking to me.... She was talking to someone who was standing in front of her.'

Chapter Thirty-Four

Tuesday 17th November – 10:15

Evason arrived at ten-fifteen. Her meeting from this morning energised her. Jamieson let her open the briefing; otherwise, he thought, she may have figuratively burst.

'I met the most amazing woman this morning,' she said: 'never underestimate the little people or do so at your peril.'

She put her phone on the table and turned it up as loudly as possible. 'Listen to this,' she almost demanded, 'Tell me what you hear.'

It was a recording of the emergency call made by Holly Matthews.

They listened.

When it had finished, Stone said: 'The emergency call. Very well dealt with by the call handler, but what about it?'

'Listen again.' Said Evason.

They listened again.

Still nothing from Jamieson, Stone and Johnson. 'This is brilliant.' Buzzed Evason. 'The difference between listening and hearing, I never realised the importance before.'

This time she played the shortened version that Mary had played to her.

Still puzzled and then Johnson said, a little uncertainly, 'it feels as though 'Move' is a strange word to use in the context of that conversation, I mean to someone dealing with an emergency call. You would say, 'Hurry up' or 'get a move on'. But 'Move' is what you would say to someone standing in front of you.' He used his hand to indicate an invisible person standing three yards away.

Evason's eyes widened, and a huge grin crept across her face.

Jamieson nodded slowly: 'That is exactly what she is doing, isn't it? She's not talking to the operator; she's talking to someone standing with her. She wasn't alone; someone was with her, wasn't there?'

Evason nodded: 'It certainly seems that way.'

She then explained Mary's theory about why the words 'Move, move' sounded quieter than the rest of the conversation.

'She's talking into the mouthpiece, then moves it away to speak to the person with her - move, move - then brings it back to the mouthpiece to continue the conversation with the emergency services team.' All the time, Evason mimes what she believes has happened.

'That's astonishing', said Stone 'you could have played me that recording a hundred times, and I wouldn't have heard the significance, but now you explain it, it's bloody obvious. We need to second this call handler to the team; she'll run rings around us all!'

He laughed and shook his head: 'Astonishing', he repeated.

'So, what now?' asked Johnson.

Jamieson thought about the conversation with the Chief Constable yesterday evening: Would this constitute more evidence in his book? But, thought Jamieson, it wasn't his book that mattered during a live investigation; it would be the officer in charge, and that was him, Jamieson.

'We knew there was a connection between Holly and Mcniven, but we didn't know what. With what we've learned, it's fair to say that the connection is not a what but, more likely, a who.' He shrugged: 'Let's bring them in again.'

Jamieson knew he was taking a risk and that Jarman would not be happy if it went wrong. But life was about taking risks.

Chapter Thirty-Five

Tuesday 17th November - 11:10

Mrs Matthews closed the front door behind her so the girls inside could not hear her.

Her voice was lowered, which made her sound more aggressive, more menacing, if indeed that were possible: 'You fucking people don't know what you're doing.' She hissed. 'You had her there for nearly eight hours yesterday and let her go. Now you want her back again. She is grieving for the loss of her son; don't you bastards get that?'

Evason stood firm: 'I did say yesterday that if she answered our questions, then it would be much easier for us to find out who was responsible for her son's death; she didn't answer them. Some more information has come to light that we need to ask her about. The same rules apply as yesterday; if she chooses to answer them, then we can do our jobs properly. If she chooses not to, we can't. All pretty straightforward. Is she ready yet?'

Mcniven, again, was far more straightforward. He was at the club doing paperwork. He looked almost resigned

when the officers were shown into the office. They explained that he was required back at the station. Mcniven
took his jacket from the back of the chair, slipped it on and
followed them to the car. It was as if he was waiting for
them.

Anna Chaston, the solicitor, was as put out as Jamieson
had ever seen her: 'Jesus, Alex,' she said. 'You only let them
go fifteen hours ago, yet here we are back again. I've got
work on my desk that won't get done by itself.'

'Sorry Anna, some fresh information has come to light',
explained Jamieson. He really wasn't sorry.

This time Holly and Mcniven were put in the opposite
interview rooms to where they were yesterday. No reason.

The team met for a briefing before tackling the interviews.

Similarly to yesterday, it would be Evason and Johnson
in with Holly, Jamieson, and Stone with Mcniven. Jamieson
knew that if anything were going to give, it would be Mcniv-
en. He was their weak link. Holly would bat questions back
until the proverbial cows came home. Mcniven was weaker
and more emotional. If Jamieson got his questioning right
and cranked up the pressure, he would get what he needed
from Mcniven. He was sure of it.

Both interviews started precisely as they had yesterday.
They covered all the points previously raised. Holly was
more controlled today and gave a 'no comment' to everything fired at her. Anna Chaston seemed more relaxed.

Mcniven was still twitchy. He blustered a bit, but on the
whole, his answers were the same as they had been. He'd
been at the club until he left for his shift at the supermarket. He couldn't remember who had called him. He'd put

his coat on to change a barrel and returned shortly after. He first knew of Ashley's death when someone walked into the bar just before nine o'clock and told everyone. That was it. That was all he could remember.

Evason spoke: 'Holly, we have reason to believe that Ashley was not alone when you found him. So who was with him, Holly? Who were you speaking to?'

Holly, defiant: 'no comment'. She laughed a short, sharp bark. Then, she leaned across the table towards Evason: 'I was alone with my son; what don't you get about that?'

Evason checked *her* watch: eleven twenty precisely.

Jamieson checked *his* watch: eleven twenty precisely.

Evason leaned forward towards Holly. There were inches between their faces: 'Holly, it was Lewis, who you were speaking to, wasn't it? Lewis Killed Ashley, didn't he?'

Jamieson looked at Mcniven: 'Davey, Lewis is your son, isn't he? You cheated on your friend, Jason, with his girlfriend while he was away, didn't you? Where is he, Davey? Where is Lewis?'

Chapter Thirty-Six

Tuesday 17th November – 17:30

Lewis Matthews was nearly fourteen, but sitting opposite Jamieson in the same interview room his mother had occupied two hours previously, he looked nearer to eleven or twelve.

Jamieson's hunch had paid off. The absence of Lewis had troubled him from the very beginning. Why had the family shuffled him well away from things when his brother had been killed? To protect him? Maybe. But wouldn't a family dominated by the overbearing matriarchal presence of Holly's Mother draw itself closer, effectively inwards on itself, rather than spreading itself wider?

Was it a case of out of sight being out of mind for the boy?

On balance, what reason would Holly Matthews have for phoning Davey Mcniven not five minutes after her son had been stabbed? Nothing obvious, and yet.......Jamieson's brain kept taking him back to Lewis.

And that was where Jamieson ended up.

Throw all the ingredients into the mix and see what comes out. So, in went Holly Matthews, Davey Mcniven, Ashley Matthews, Lewis Matthews, Jason James and Michael Macklin.

As far as Jamieson was concerned, Macklin was always a convenient fall guy, so he quickly discounted him. Jason James too. Although he was part of the jigsaw, there was no connection between him and what happened that evening. So that left Davey, Holly, Ashley and Lewis. Jamieson had played around with the combinations, and the only one that made sense was that Holly and Davey were the biological parents of Lewis. Is that who they were protecting?

Only one way to find out.

Mcniven's reaction to Jamieson's straightforward question was compelling. His face crumpled, and his sobs told Jamieson all that he needed to know. His hunch was correct. Lewis was his son. Now he needed to speak to the boy as quickly as possible to get his undiluted version of events.

'He's with my parents', said Mcniven. 'they live in Welwyn Garden City.' Welwyn was about thirteen miles from Luton.

'So,' said Jamieson, looking for confirmation, 'Holly called you, and then what?'

Mcniven sniffed: 'She just said to get Lewis away from here, that something big had gone down and Lewis needed to be somewhere else. So I said I could take him to my parent's house, and she said that was fine. I was to come to her place on Thursday afternoon, and she would tell me more. She said to meet Lewis on the corner of Holmes Road and Bedford Road and take him to my parents for a few days, and then I was to come back and act as if nothing had happened. Also, I shouldn't tell Lewis anything I didn't need to.'

Jamieson checked his watch: two thirty. He needed to get to Welwyn to collect Lewis and get him back here as soon as possible.

'Ok, Davey, ' he said, pushing a piece of paper and pen across the desk to him. 'I need you to write down your parents' address for me. Mcniven did as he was asked.

He looked Mcniven directly in the eye: 'So I am going to drive over to Welwyn now and bring Lewis back with me.'

'When I get there, I will need you to phone your parents and explain who I am and that I must take Lewis back with me. I won't be alone.' He indicated Evason sitting to his left: 'DS Evason will be with me, and we will take an appropriate adult with us to make Lewis feel more at ease. Do you understand that, Davey?'

Mcniven nodded and sniffed again.

Jamieson pressed the stop button on the recorder: 'Interview suspended.' He announced.

With Mcniven back in the holding cell, Jamieson instructed Evason to find the best appropriate adult available immediately and arrange for a pool car they could use to drive across to Welwyn. Very quickly and with her usual efficiency, Evason arranged for the appropriate adult, fifty-four-year-old Alison Hedges, a part-time teaching assistant. An excellent choice, thought Jamieson.

Alison Hedges was with them within fifteen minutes, and within five minutes, they had set out on the short journey to Welwyn. On the way, Evason outlined the situation to Alison Hedges. By coincidence, she had worked in Lewis's school and had previously had some contact with him.

'That's very helpful,' thought Jamieson, a familiar face for the lad to latch onto.'

As it was, the transition was all very smooth. Mcniven did his part. His parents, whilst very confused about the whole situation, were compliant. Jamieson wondered whether they were aware that the boy they had looked after for the past few days was actually their grandson or whether they had just done what their son had asked without question. Maybe they suspected; all irrelevant now, though, thought Jamieson.

The journey there and back had taken no more than two hours. The same individuals in the car were sitting in the interview room with the appointed duty solicitor.

Lewis had a bag of crisps and a glass of orange squash on the table in front of him. He did not look nervous, perhaps more excited.

However, it was evident from his demeanour that he was unaware that Ashley was dead. It almost felt like he was looking forward to seeing his brother to tell him about this new adventure.

Mrs Hedges spoke to Lewis. She explained that Jamieson would ask him some questions, and it was important that he tried to answer them as honestly as possible.

Lewis asked if he could eat his crisps because he was hungry. 'Of course, you can.' Replied Mrs Hedges. He opened his crisps, and Mrs Hedges asked if he was ready. Lewis said that he was, and the interview began.

'Hello, Lewis.' Said, Jamieson. 'My name is Alex. I see you like football.' He said, pointing at the boy's shirt. 'Which team is that?'

'Luton Town.' Replied Lewis. 'I don't really support them, but they are my third-best team.'

'I see', said Jamieson. 'Your brother Ashley likes football, doesn't he? He's a good player, I've heard.'

Lewis visibly pushed his chest out with pride: 'He's great. He's going to play for England.'

'Tell me about him, Lewis.' Prompted Jamieson.

'He plays for Akley FC, but soon he will play for a big team, that's what his Dad Jason says. He won't say who, just that it is a big team. Ash says that when he signs, everything will change. He says I won't have to go to school anymore because he will have so much money that we can buy a big house and live there together with his Dad and the girls. And he can pay for Mum to go to hospital so she will get better, and then she can live with us as well.'

'What about your Nan?' asked Jamieson.

Lewis looked at Mrs Hedges anxiously: 'Can I swear?' He whispered. She nodded.

'Ash doesn't like Nan because she doesn't like his Dad. So he says she can..' he mouthed the words 'fuck off' and pulled a face. 'When he said that, we would always giggle because we aren't allowed to swear, really.'

'Do you like Jason, Lewis?' asked Jamieson.

'Yes', answered Lewis, 'but he's not my Dad. Jason is black, and I'm not, so he can't be my Dad. I don't know who my Dad is. Mum says the papers have got lost. Whenever Jason came over from Spain to see Ash, he would also take me out. He bought me this football shirt.' He pulled at the badge over his left breast. 'And Ash bought me some trainers.' He smiled.

'How is school, Lewis?' Said, Jamieson.

"It's ok, but I don't really like it.'

'Why is that?'

Lewis pulled a face: 'Well, there are some big kids there, and they kept saying that Ash wasn't going to be a footballer. They said he's in a gang and that he will get stabbed soon, and then he wouldn't be able to be a footballer anymore.'

'How did that make you feel, Lewis?' Continued Jamieson.

'I told them to shut up, but they wouldn't. Of course, Ash is going to be a footballer. If he weren't, then we wouldn't be able to buy a big house, and all live in it, and Ash wouldn't lie about things like that. Not to me.'

'What happened then, Lewis?'

'One night when he went out, I sneaked out after him and followed him.'

'Where did he go?'

Lewis looked concerned like he did not want to get his big brother into trouble. 'He met with some older kids who I didn't recognise. I had to go home then because it was getting late, and I knew Mum and Nan would be looking for me.'

Jamieson waited. He was experienced enough to know that a good silence was worth a thousand words.

Lewis continued: 'They were so mad when I got home. Nan really shouted at me. Then they put something on my phone, so they knew where I was whenever I had my phone with me.'

Jamieson looked at Evason. The tracking software on Holly's phone wasn't tracking Ashley but Lewis. It was Lewis that she was tracking that night.

'What happened next, Lewis?' asked Jamieson gently.

Lewis looked upset, and both the solicitor and the appropriate adult had looks of concern on their faces. Jamieson knew that the interview had reached a critical point, and they needed to push on from here.

'Are you ok, Lewis?' He asked.

Lewis gritted his teeth and continued: 'It looked like the big kids at school were right, Ash was in a gang, and I didn't understand why he was going to be a big footballer. He was going to play for England and buy us all a big house, and he would mess it all up if he were in a gang. I didn't understand why. Didn't he love us? Didn't he want us all to be together?'

'Then what happened?' asked Jamieson. He leaned forward, elbows on the table, hands together under his chin.

'I spoke to him about it, but he just said not to worry, but the kids at school kept going on about him being stabbed up because he was in a gang, and he kept going out every night to meet those other older kids. I was really scared.'

Jamieson lowered his voice almost to a whisper: 'Then what, Lewis?'

'I had an idea.' Said the boy. 'I thought that if Ash got a little injury, he would see what he was doing was dangerous, which might stop him from being a footballer. So, I followed him a couple of nights later. I took a knife from the kitchen. I thought if I gave him, like, a little stab in the leg that wasn't too bad, then he'd know how upset I was, and he would stop being in the gang, and everything would be alright again.'

'I followed him, caught up with him and called his name out. He turned around and smiled. He said not to worry. He would only be doing this for another few weeks just to sort mum out and that I should go home before I got into trouble. He wasn't angry. He never got angry with me, Ash.'

'I took the knife out and held it in front of me. Ash said, " Come on, Bro, let's put that away before someone gets hurt, but I still thought my plan would work. I pushed the knife forward to give him a little stab in the leg, but he had moved forward to take the knife from me, so the knife went in deeper than I meant. He was wearing his grey Nike track bottoms, and some blood came through quite quickly, but he was ok; he was standing in front of me. He wasn't angry with me; he knew what I meant to do, and he wasn't angry with me.'

'Then Mum was there, and suddenly Ash was on the floor. Mum was crying. The patch of blood on Ash's track bottoms had got bigger. Mum phoned someone and told me to hide the knife up my sleeve and walk along the street until I reached the end of the road and that someone would pick me up from there and take me somewhere safe for a few days.'

'Did you go straight away?' Asked Jamieson.

'No, I couldn't make my legs work. Mum phoned someone else and was talking to them and looked up and noticed I was still standing there. She shouted move or go or something like that, and pointed down the road. This time my legs worked, so I walked down to where she told me and waited. A car came, and a man told me to get in, so I did.'

'Do you know where he took you?' Said, Jamieson.

'We went to a house with two old people in it. They were nice to me, but they took my phone and switched it off.

The man who drove me there didn't stay very long.' Lewis paused, and a thought crossed his mind.

'Was he my Dad?' He finally asked.

Chapter Thirty-Seven

Tuesday 17th November – 18:15

The feeling back in the operations room was very flat.

It was six fifteen.

Stone spoke: 'So the kid doesn't know that his big brother is dead, or more specifically, that he killed his big brother?'

Typical directness from Stone. Although he was technically correct in that Lewis was responsible for the death of Ashley, Jamieson wished he had used a different way to express what they were all thinking. No-one answered.

'What now?' Continued Stone.

Jamieson scratched his head. 'It's out of our hands. We've provided a solution which is what we were asked to do. It's in the hands of the CPS now. Lewis will undergo a psychological examination, and the outcome will decide what happens from there.'

'For what it's worth,' He continued, 'I believe every word he's just told us. I honestly think he thought that his plan would shock Ashley into seeing sense, but in the end, he was just plain unlucky.' He recalled the pathologist Tilly

Jenner's words about the protection that surrounded the femoral artery, what with bone, sinew and muscle in abundance in that area and just how incredible it was that the point of Lewis' knife missed everything and found its way to the artery.

Evason was very quiet. She was sitting forward at her desk with her elbows on the surface, her chin buried in her clenched fists. Johnson was equally subdued. He was perched on the edge of his desk.

There was none of the usual euphorias when a significant case had been cracked. Instead, it felt like a very hollow victory.

'How do you see the rest of it, Alex?' Asked Stone.

Jamieson gave a slight shrug: 'Well,' he said, 'When Holly came across the two boys, she was pretty quick to assess the situation. One of her sons, Ashley, with blood dripping from his leg, and the other, Lewis, holding a knife. It was pretty evident what had happened, although she may not have realised why it had happened. Her first thought was getting Lewis out of the way, so she phoned Mcniven, the boy's father, and told him to get Lewis as far away from the scene as possible. Then she phoned emergency services. What we don't know is whether that delay, while she phoned Mcniven, proved critical in Ashley's death. As they often say, timing is everything. Mcniven picked the boy up and took him to his parent's house in Welwyn. He told them to take his phone and not switch it on. Holly then phoned the emergency services, so they probably lost, what, a minute or two getting to Ashley. Her problem was her phone. The ambulance crew had seen her with it when they first arrived on the scene, and she had no opportunity of getting rid of it without being seen. Her only option was to try as best she could to smash it up and hide it somewhere in the ambulance.' He shrugged: 'And as we know, that didn't work.'

'Holly understandably lost the plot when she got to the hospital and discovered that Ashley had died from his injuries. She'd lost one son; the other could face a long spell in a juvenile offenders' unit. So, she clammed up apart from sticking to her story of finding Ashley injured.'

'That's where Mrs Matthews gets involved. My guess is that the three of them, Mrs Matthews, Holly and Mcniven, got together sometime on the Thursday to get their story straight. Holly suddenly remembers that she saw Michael Macklin, and Mcniven says that he was a thug who was kicked out of the football club. Mrs Matthews sees an opportunity. If Macklin were in the vicinity, perhaps they could pin Ashley's stabbing on him. Mcniven confirmed that he'd got a record for possessing a knife so that all conveniently fell into place.'

Stone spoke: 'So Macklin was going to be their fall guy? He was going to have the blame for what happened?'

'It's conjecture, but it fits.' said Jamieson

'But why the attack on Macklin?' asked Johnson.

'Well, he was a loose end, and if he weren't taken care of, the story might all unravel, and we'd be inclined to look deeper at things. But, as it happens, Jason James turned up on the Friday, and Holly was sure to tell him she had seen Macklin near where Ashley had been attacked. So when Sandy and Claire visited on the Saturday morning, the Michael Macklin line was reinforced. Then Claire received a call from Mrs Matthews on Sunday morning, again re-reinforcing Macklin's name and putting Jason James in the picture as a violent, coercive individual who could easily be hell-bent on revenge.'

Evason spoke: 'I did feel as though I were being played', she said.

Jamieson continued: 'We've now got Mcniven's phone records which show he spoke to Jason James for thirty-five minutes on Sunday afternoon. Now clearly, we don't know what the conversation was about. Still, if we were to ask Mcniven, he would say they talked about Macklin and how he might be responsible for Ash's death. He would also say that Jason got very riled up and said he would see that Macklin didn't wreck anyone else's life. By the way, I don't think that happened, but Mcniven would tell us that it did again to give us a picture of Jason's state of mind.'

'Then, in all likelihood, Mcniven went and waited outside Macklin's local and pulped his head in with a baseball bat. Well, that seems most likely.'

'So, the story that they were trying to spin was that Michael Macklin murdered Ashley, and then Macklin was reduced to a vegetable by Ashley's grieving father?' said Johnson.

Jamieson nodded.

'I suppose there's method in there somewhere', said Stone. 'By the way, how can you be so sure that it was Mcniven who beat Macklin up.'

Jamieson took a deep breath in and puffed his cheeks out: 'Well, Sandy,' he said, 'you know as well as I do that police work is a lot of hard hours and graft, and sometimes that is followed by just the tiniest bit of luck.....' Stone nodded. '......we impounded Mcniven's car a couple of hours ago. In the boot, there's a blooded baseball bat with prints and DNA all over it, probably Mcniven's. The blood is being tested as to type for Michael Macklin. We also found a kitchen knife which is also being tested. Pretty sure it'll be Ashley's blood type and Lewis' DNA. It seems that Davey Mcniven doesn't watch television detective shows and didn't realise that he needed to dispose of all the evidence.'

Chapter Thirty-Eight

Tuesday 17th November – 18:50

Jamieson found a parking spot near the address Jason James had provided them with for his stay in the UK.

He checked his watch – six fifty – it was dark, although the rain that had beaten down for the past six days had now reduced to a fine drizzle.

He found the house he was looking for, went up the garden path and pressed the doorbell.

A light appeared inside the property hallway, and a figure appeared behind the frosted glass. Jamieson had his warrant card out, ready.

A black lady opened the door, Jamieson guessed, in her sixties. She stood tall and proud and had an attractive face. She wore a black dress with a grey cardigan over her shoulders. Her arms were folded across her bosom.

Jamieson showed his warrant card; 'Hello,' he said, 'I was looking for Jason.'

She nodded slowly. 'I hope he's not in trouble,' she said, smiling sadly to let Jamieson know she was joking. 'He's upstairs in the shower.' She stepped back and held her arm out, inviting him in. 'You're more than welcome to wait.'

'I will, thank you.' Said Jamieson stepping over the threshold. He followed her through to the kitchen.

It was a small house, but well looked after by someone who took pride in it.

There was a packed suitcase in the hallway, which Jamieson skirted around.

The kitchen was surprisingly large and housed a table with four chairs and the usual appliances in that particular room.

She offered Jamieson a seat.

'I'm Jason's Mother', she explained somewhat unnecessarily, 'Martha.' She offered her hand. Jamieson stood up and shook it. He noticed that her fingernails were well-manicured. She wore a wedding band. Jamieson remembered Jason saying that his father had died a few years previously.

And now she was grieving the death of her grandson.

He looked her in the eye: 'I'm so sorry for your loss.' He said.

Martha nodded: 'Yes.' She said: 'Yes. So awful. Such a young man.' There was a sadness in her eyes as if she couldn't bring herself to accept what had happened, although she had no option.

'Will you take tea?' she asked. 'That's what we do in times of stress, isn't it? Drink tea?' she smiled.

'I will, thank you.' Said, Jamieson.

Martha filled the kettle and flicked the switch to 'on'.

'Excuse me,' she said and went out into the hallway. Jamieson could hear a muffled conversation.

Martha came back in: 'He's just finishing up', She explained, 'he'll be another five minutes.'

She made the tea.

With her back turned to Jamieson, she asked: 'Are you allowed to tell me if there have been any developments?'

'There have, he replied. 'Do you mind if we wait until Jason gets down to discuss them? Better for you to both hear at the same time.'

Martha turned and handed him his tea: 'I've assumed milk, no sugar.'

'Lovely, thanks', replied Jamieson. Martha put a mug of tea on the table for when Jason came down. She sat opposite Jamieson with her drink.

Jamieson didn't know what to say, and there was a moment of awkwardness. Then, finally, he spoke: 'Tough week?' he said.

He knew it was stupid to say but had nothing better at that moment.

Martha gave another sad smile. Jamieson thought she had probably been doing that a lot over the past week or so. 'I lost my husband ten years ago,' she said. 'And I thought that was the worst thing I would ever experience. But this.....' She momentarily paused. She put her hand up to her chest. '....but this, this is another level of hurt. For God's sake, he was sixteen.'

Jamieson felt this was the type of woman who did not take the Lord's name in vain lightly.

Another silence filled the air between the two of them. Jamieson was just about to speak when the door opened.

Jason James came in. He held his right hand above shoulder height. His index finger was wrapped in tissue. There was blood on the tissue.

'Alex,' He said, offering his left hand, which Jamieson shook, 'Sorry, I was in the shower.' He turned to his Mother. 'Mum, that cut has opened up again. Have you got a plaster handy?'

Martha stood: 'In the bathroom.' She said, pushing past him to get there. 'Your tea is there on the table.'

Jason sat down. 'What have you done?' asked Jamieson, indicating Jason's finger with an incline of his head.

'Ah, just caught it on something the other day.' Answered Jason. Martha came back in. Jason held his hand up, and Martha wrapped the sticking plaster around the tip of his finger. Jamieson smiled to himself. It seemed that Mums would always be Mums, and sons would always be sons.

Martha sat down and said, 'Inspector Jamieson has some news.' She said to Jason.

Jason looked at him expectantly.

Jamieson was not one for drama.

'A horrible accident', he said. 'It seems that his half-brother Lewis is responsible.'

Martha put her hand to her mouth.

'Lewis?' said Jason. 'The kid couldn't hurt a fly.'

Jamieson recounted the situation almost in full. He made no mention of Michael Macklin.

Tears slid down Martha's face: 'So Ashley was mixed up with gangs and drugs?' She looked helplessly at Jamieson.

Jason interrupted: 'Yes, but only because Holly had fucked up and got behind with the rent and everything else.

Isn't that right, Alex?' He desperately sought Jamieson's confirmation.

Jamieson considered his answer: 'Yes, he was in a gang and yes, as far as I could see, the reason he did it was to keep the family together and get them out of a hole. As I said, there were massive rent arrears, and the family had been threatened with eviction; whether right or wrong, Ashley's actions got them out of that situation and held the family together.'

'Lewis came under pressure at school and thought that Ashley getting mixed up with drugs would stop him from becoming a footballer. So he planned to scare Ashley into seeing sense, and, well, we know what happened then.'

Jason buried his face in his hands. Gradually emerging as he drew them downwards past his chin.

Jamieson waited whilst everyone regained their composure.

'Were you aware that Davey Mcniven was Lewis' father?' He asked Jason.

Jason looked at him: 'Suspected it,' he said, 'but never had it confirmed either way.'

He continued: 'When I first went to Spain and was away for three weeks at a time, I asked Mcniven to watch out for Holly. I considered him a mate, but he was a weak bloke. He used to latch onto people and follow them around like a little puppy. Within a couple of months, Holly had gone back to her old ways. Mcniven wouldn't have been a match for a pissed-up, coked-up Holly. When she was like that, she got what she wanted. She probably wanted some male attention one night, and Mcniven was johnny on the spot, as it were. She would have eaten him up and spat him out. He wouldn't have stood a chance.'

'It was obvious when Lewis was born that I wasn't his Dad.' He stopped talking and seemed to be considering something. 'I couldn't deal with it, so I upped and left. Threw money at the situation, hoping that that would sort it out.'

He continued: 'You know that Ash could've signed pro forms on his sixteenth birthday. That would have given them more than enough to live on. There would have been no rent arrears then.'

'But I said 'no''. Jason gave a little shrug and opened his hands in front of him. 'Because of what happened to me, I said 'no'. But everything was different. Ash was a bloody brilliant footballer, whereas I was average at best, and football has changed so much since then. You aren't just cut adrift these days if you aren't considered good enough anymore. There's support from the club, opportunities to retrain.'

Martha put her hand on Jason's: 'Don't do this to yourself,' she said. 'It won't bring Ashley back.'

Jason looked at his Mother. His eyes shone with tears. 'But I failed him, Mum, I failed him twice. First, I left him on his own, and then, when he had an opportunity to lift himself and everyone around him out of the shit they were in, I said 'no'. What sort of a Father would do that?'

Martha grabbed both of Jason's hands: 'Look at me.' She demanded. 'Look at me. Life is about making decisions. When you made both of those decisions, you gave them due consideration and made the right decisions for the right reasons. Ashley died because of a freak set of circumstances, not because of some decisions you made for what you believed was best for the family. For God's sake, Jason, he'd still be with us if Lewis had picked up a smaller knife or if the knife hadn't found the thousand-to-one gap that it did. It was a horrible, horrible situation, but it could not be avoided. Do not blame yourself. Do not feel pity for yourself; that is not how you were bought up.'

As quickly as the situation had escalated, a relative calm settled in the room.

Jason sat. His shoulders rose and fell with his quiet sobbing.

Martha spoke: 'What will happen to Lewis now?' She asked.

This time Jamieson gave a slight shrug: 'Phycological tests, involvement of Social Services and the Courts. I don't think he will be charged with murder or even manslaughter. My guess is that it is more likely to be a charge of possession and some time spent in a juvenile facility.'

Martha cleared her throat: 'I met the boy occasionally. He adored Ashley. If he needs a character reference of any kind, I won't hesitate,' she looked to Jason, 'and neither would Jason.'

Jamieson nodded. In his career, he had encountered some exceptional people, and although he had only known Martha briefly, he had no doubt that she was right up there with the best of them.

Jason sniffed: 'What about Holly and Mcniven?' he asked.

'Um,' said Jamieson ', The Crown Prosecution Service are looking at them, possibly perverting the course of justice, harbouring a criminal, that sort of thing. Unlikely that Holly will get a custodial sentence, given the girls. Mcniven maybe more so, but anything is likely to be suspended.'

Jamieson felt like adding that he didn't attach too much blame to Holly and Mcniven for their part in the cover-up. But, on the other hand, you had to ask yourself what you would do if one of your sons or daughters found themselves in a similar situation. What would it have been if your instinct was not to try to make it right for them?

Jamieson stood to leave.

Martha offered her hand. When Jamieson took it, she covered his hand with her other hand. Then, she simply said: 'Thank you.'

Jamieson just nodded. There wasn't much more to say.

On the way through the hall, Jamieson indicated the packed suitcase. 'Yours?' He asked Jason.

Jason nodded: 'I fly back first thing in the morning.'

'And then back for the funeral?' Asked Jamieson.

This time Jason shook his head. 'No', he said and shrugged. 'Mum will be my representative at the funeral. I don't think I could do it. I know people talk about closure and goodbyes....' He touched his chest '....Ash is in here. There will never be closure, and a funeral isn't going to change that. I don't want to be around Holly and her Mother; I might do something I would regret.'

Jason opened the front door and ushered Jamieson out. He offered his left hand on the doorstep, and Jamieson grasped it in his own.

'Look after that finger', said Jamieson before turning and walking down the garden path.

When he reached the gate, Jason called out, and Jamieson turned.

'Michael Macklin.' Asked Jason. 'What was his involve-ment in all this?'

'Well,' said Jamieson ', He did meet Ash on the night Ash died, but it seems like a coincidence. I think that perhaps Holly and her Mother were trying to make more of the meeting than there actually was. Ironically, it seems that Macklin thought Ash was a good friend. Really appreciated his company.'

'I heard that someone gave Macklin a beating.' Said, Jason.

'Yes', said Jamieson. 'He's in a bad way. We're looking at Mcniven for that, but it could just be another coincidence – Macklin is a pretty objectionable individual – there could be any number of suspects.'

Jason nodded and raised his hand in goodbye, a gesture which Jamieson reciprocated.

Jamieson pulled the gate closed behind him and checked his watch – seven-thirty - he would call Lucy on the way home, and they would go through the takeaway/pasta scenario. But tonight, he was tired and hungry and had just closed an important case. He felt the least he deserved was a curry.

Chapter Thirty-Nine

Saturday 11th December – 19:15

Claire Evason looked at herself in the mirror and approved.

She turned sideways on and smoothed herself down.

She only sometimes went to this much effort. She wore her same unofficial uniform of jeans, a t-shirt and jacket and flat pumps or trainers for work. Never would she ever contemplate wearing make-up of any kind for work. It just wasn't her style.

But tonight was different.

Tonight, she would, for the first time, be seeing Pete Jarman, her secret partner of the last two years, in public. Okay, so they wouldn't be a couple, but they would be at a work party at the same time, and that was a start. They had discussed engineering a way of leaving at the same time, not in an obvious way, but in a 'sharing a cab home' type of way.

Claire had been looking forward to this evening since Jamieson had told them about it. And, if things went well, she might even broach the subject of Jarman, actually considering their relationship to be serious and one that had a future away from faraway restaurants and discreet hotel rooms.

Claire wore skinny jeans and a black t-shirt with her ankle-length suede boots. In addition, she would be wearing her favourite leather jacket. She had had it for ten years or so. She had bought it with her first wage packet as a lowly constable. It had eaten up most of what she had earned that month, but, she told herself, it had lasted, and the soft leather was to die for. So, all in all, a good investment.

She moved closer to the mirror and studied her face. She had used a touch of mascara, just enough to bring her eyes out, and some subtle lipstick. She stepped back. Her boobs looked good, although she always wished they were a touch bigger. She spun side onto the mirror and slapped herself on the backside with both hands.

She nodded.

She looked good this evening.

She might even turn Roger Johnson's head tonight.

Yes, she knew, but she didn't know if he knew she knew. That made her laugh; it sounded a bit sitcom-ish.

She had grown fond of her colleague since he had joined the team. He worked hard, had an excellent approach to the job, and, to boot, a good sense of humour, which was very important when dealing with the things they dealt with regularly.

She knew he was gay because she had worked with many, many male colleagues in the past and put up with their boorish behaviour, passed off as banter, put up with too many comments, not necessarily aimed at her but at members of her sex. She had put up with most of those comments up until now. Still, if anyone ever, ever overstepped the mark, she would peg them back, leaving them in no doubt that if they ever spoke like that in her presence again, she would not hesitate to file an official complaint against them.

Johnson was not like that. Neither was Jamieson, and, in fairness, even the old dinosaur, Stone, only skirted around that kind of talk to get a rise out of her.

Her phone beeped. Her cab was outside.

She pulled on her leather jacket, scooped up her shoulder bag, looked in the mirror, flicked her hair, and switched off the light.

The cab ride was ten miles, probably twenty minutes at the most. Her driver, Ravi, opened the back door, but she was having none of that and sat upfront with him. He was in his early thirties and explained that he was working this shift to help the family business. He was a trained accountant and was looking to branch out on his own.

Ravi showed an interest in Claire, and the journey was very pleasant. He was good company. As they neared their destination, Claire realised she would be very early, so she asked Ravi to drop her half a mile shy of where she had initially requested. It was a mild evening, and she loved the general feeling of the period leading up to Christmas when, for once, most people seemed happy and put their sorrows and woes on the back burner. It was, after all, the season of goodwill. So a stroll along the high street would do her good.

Ravi dropped her off and scribbled his mobile number on the back of the business card. 'Call me when you are ready to leave.' He said. 'I'll collect you personally.' He grinned.

Claire smiled. Some male interest made her feel good about herself.

She set off, and, as usual, her mind turned to work. The last case they had worked on as a team had been tough. Another young life lost to knife crime was bad enough, but the fact that it turns out that his brother was responsible somehow made it worse.

Holly Matthews and Davey Mcniven had been released but, in all likelihood, would be charged with something at some point in the future. Lewis was still under the social services team. When he was finally told that Ashley had died from his wounds, he became distraught and had to be sedated to calm him down. Since then, he had been kept in a secure juvenile facility under observation and pending the charging decision. He was a kid and did not really know what was happening. Claire felt it was all very sad.

Michael Macklin had come out of his coma. He was still in a bad way but strong, and doctors hoped he would regain most of his faculties.

The original theory that Davey Mcniven was responsible for the attack had proved without merit. Although the baseball bat had been found in the boot of his car, there was no evidence to connect him to it. Furthermore, it was common knowledge that he didn't lock the trunk, so anyone had access to it to plant whatever they wanted.

Additionally, Michael Macklin confirmed that the attacker was not Mcniven. He knew Mcniven from his time at Akley FC, and, as much as he disliked the man, he was adamant that it was not him with the baseball bat that night. Given the battering that Macklin had taken, Claire wondered how he could be so sure, but he was, and the police had to accept that.

There were a few loose ends. There were some tiny drops of blood just inside the trunk of Mcniven's car – it seemed possible that whoever had planted the baseball bat had injured themselves on the lock and shed some blood – initial DNA tests had ruled Mcniven out and anyone else on the database for a direct match. Jamieson had asked for testing for a familial match – tests against the database for a close family member to be carried out – this wasn't as precise as a direct match and was expensive to carry out, so it had to be signed off, ironically for Claire, by the Chief Constable. The last Claire had heard, it had been agreed, and testing would begin as soon as physically possible.

After a pleasant fifteen-minute walk, she reached the Bell pub – a vast, sprawling old-fashioned type of establishment – and the car park outside was packed. There were people everywhere; perhaps she had underestimated this event and how popular it would be.

She went up to the entrance and presented her ticket. The young man stamped her hand, 'for readmission,' he explained, and she went through to a sizeable entertaining venue. The crowd looked already well over a hundred, and the throng of people's voices over the backdrop of music gave Claire a real buzz.

Jamieson had told them that Lucy would be there early and secure a table to the right of the stage near the front, which they could congregate at and use as a base. Claire tiptoed and, over the heads of the crowd, caught sight of Lucy and headed in that direction.

Claire had met Lucy at several social events and enjoyed her company. They were cut from the same cloth and invariably giggled their way through some stuffy old police work events – tonight would be different, she felt sure.

As Claire approached, Lucy spotted her and jumped up. She stepped back and surveyed Claire: 'My God, DS Evason, you scrub up well; even I fancy you tonight!' And she gathered Claire into her arms for a heartfelt hug.

Claire stepped out of the hug and smiled: 'Well, Mrs Jamieson,' she said, looking Lucy up and down, 'the same could be said of you, absolutely stunning.'

'Wow', thought Claire ', Lucy was, what, forty-five, forty-six; if I look anything like that when I'm that age, I'll be delighted.' DI Jamieson was a fortunate man.

'Ok', said Lucy. 'First things first. Alex has put some money behind the bar, so get whatever you want....' They both looked towards the heaving bar, currently three deep. '....or I've got a cheeky bottle of white wine down here, and I'm willing to share.....'

Claire grinned: 'Wine, it is then. When the others arrive, we'll send them up to the bar for a few gin and tonics.'

Lucy grabbed a wine glass from the table and poured a good measure. She handed it to Claire: 'Cheers', she said. Lucy offered her glass. Claire clinked and said, 'Cheers' back ', here's to a good evening.'

'Ah,' said Lucy ', You won't know these two.' She pointed to two lads sitting at the table. No introduction was necessary; Claire found herself looking at two stages in the evolution of Alex Jamison. 'Xander and Jus, ' and then as an aside to Claire ', Alex dragged them along tonight; I think they're bored already.' She giggled.

Jus looked up from his phone and smiled before quickly returning to whatever he was doing. Xander, slightly older, stood and formally offered Claire his hand, which she shook: 'Lovely to meet you.' He said, unleashing a dazzling smile that told Claire he would not want for whatever company he wanted to keep at university.

Claire felt a tentative tap on her shoulder and turned to see Roger Johnson standing there.

'Hello Claire', he said, leaning in and kissing her on the cheek, which she found endearing. Perhaps she was mellowing. She wouldn't usually have felt that was appropriate from a work colleague. 'This is my friend, David.' Roger held his hand open in an introductory manner.

Introductions over, David headed off to the bar for beers for himself and Roger and another bottle of Wine for the girls.

When he was far enough away, Claire smiled at Roger: 'He's very nice.' She said and then returned the earlier compliment and leaned into him and whispered in his ear. 'If he's not your type, perhaps you could pass him onto me.'

Roger beamed: 'Oh, he's my type, alright. Keep your eyes off. Impressive work, though; clearly, you're a detective for a reason.'

They all squeezed in around the table. Claire checked her watch: eight-thirty. The main event would start at any moment now. They talked about everything and nothing; David talked to Xander about university life and expressed regret that he never went himself; Xander told him it wasn't too late and that there were plenty of mature students where he was at Birmingham. Roger talked to Lucy like they were old friends rather than two people who had met twenty minutes ago.

Claire felt good. The first two glasses of Wine had gone down well, and she was looking forward to the entertainment and seeing Jarman.

In her pocket, her phone buzzed to announce a text had been received. With a great effort, she managed to slide the phone out of her front left pocket – boy, these really were skinny jeans – before she could read the first text, a second buzzed its arrival.

They were both from 'P':

'Something's come up, can't make it, sorry' followed by 'Have you given that Met job any further thought? I need to go back to him.'

Claire's first two thoughts were: 'fuck you, you don't know what you've missed out on tonight' followed by 'Yes, and the answer is no, I'm staying with the team at Bedford.'

Her immediate thoughts were how soon she could extricate herself from where she was, get herself home, and sulk and wallow in self-pity.

Her thoughts were interrupted by someone calling her name.

She looked up and saw Mary, the call handler on the Ashley James case whose input had meant so much to get the case to a conclusion. Mary was beaming at her, beckoning her over. Claire excused herself from the group and, despite her disappointment, gave Mary a huge hug. It seemed Mary was a rocker, decked out in denim and wearing a Christmas hat.

'Thanks so much for getting us these tickets. This is right up our street. It's the last evening Geoff and I have got off together right up until Christmas Eve, and we really couldn't think of a better way to spend it. We love live music, especially something rocky.' Mary's effervescent mood was infectious, and Claire felt better about things.

'Where is Geoff?' She asked.

Mary pointed to the bar. 'That's him there at the bar wearing the leather jacket.'

Claire spotted him, and her jaw figuratively dropped. 'Wow, Mary, he's a silver fox. He's gorgeous; where did you find him?'

'He is lovely, isn't he? We've been together over thirty years, and every time he sees me, he kisses me and tells me he loves me.' Mary pulled a fake offended face. 'Eh, missus, you keep your eyes off. He's all mine.' She said, and they dissolved into fits of laughter.

Geoff pulled himself away from the bar with a pint and another for Mary. Mary signalled him over frantically. 'Geoff, Geoff. This is Claire. She got us the tickets.'

Geoff handed Mary her pint and smiled at Claire. 'Thanks very much; what do I owe you?'

Claire shook her head: 'Nothing. Nothing at all. Just have a fantastic evening. My boss plays rhythm guitar.' She shrugged. 'I Don't know what that means, but 'Jimmy Be Good' is his moment in the spotlight.'

'Johnny Be Goode, you daft mare', said Mary laughing: 'I don't know, kids of today!!'

Just then, they were joined by a fourth person: 'Oh', said Mary. 'This is our son, Tim; he's just moved back from the States – he's a bit of a billy-no-mates at the moment - so we've dragged him along tonight. I hope that's alright.'

Claire looked at Tim. He had his Father's looks. Dark tousled hair, a couple of days' stubble on his chin, deep brown eyes, scruffily dressed but looked good on it. 'Oh yes,' Claire thought ', that is definitely alright.'

'Come and meet everyone', she said, 'you won't remember anyone's name, but once the music starts and the alcohol kicks in, no one will care about that.'

Finally, just as the band came onstage to tune up, Stone appeared. He wore jeans and a check shirt with a jacket over the top. It occurred to Claire that it was the first time she'd seen him out of his work wear of suit, shirt and tie. He looked like she thought her older brother might look.

There had been some debate as to who Stone would bring with him. Apart from Jamieson, none of them had met Margaret, so no one would recognise her if she was his date for the evening.

The person he was with was a slim, pretty-looking lady. Recognition crossed Roger's face

'Aren't you.....' he began before Stone cut across him. 'This is Helen.' He announced and let everyone introduce themselves.

When they reached Claire for her introduction, Helen blushed: 'Were you in the car that day?' she whispered.

'Didn't hear a thing', She replied, waving her hand as if it weren't important. 'I was wearing my earphones trying to drown Sandy's ramblings out.'

Helen gave her a look of gratitude.

Then Billy Watson was at the microphone; 'Hello, Good evening and……….'

'.......welcome.' The crowd shouted back, and so it began. And it was bloody good. Even allowing for the three glasses of Wine Claire had downed, the band were bloody good.

She edged closer to Tim and watched Mary lose all inhibitions as the music carried her away. Tim spotted Claire and smiled at her. After the third song, he asked if she would like a drink, the bar was quiet then, and it was a good time to go; she said yes and had her first gin and tonic of the evening. Lucy caught her eye, tilted her head towards Tim at the bar, and made a face as if to say, 'look at you.'

After forty-five minutes, Billy Watson announced they would take a short break. The group returned to the table. By now, they had all had at least three drinks and were very animated.

Stone was talking to Roger and David. Claire heard him say, 'there must be some females in here for a couple of blokes like you.' She grinned at Roger, who smiled back. No clue, but still, Sandy was a good detective in other ways.

Mary and Geoff were talking in a group with Lucy and Helen. Alex had joined them from the stage for a couple of minutes. He was sweaty, but Mary looked at him as if he were a genuine rock star. She told him that her favourite song was 'Born to run' by Springsteen. Jamieson explained that a request slot was coming up where audience members wrote their requests on strips of paper. Billy Watson drew them out on stage, and the band would play the song if your request were drawn. Mary scuttled off to find the request slip, and Jamieson returned to the rest of the band on stage.

Claire felt good. Her earlier disappointment had crystallised her thoughts, and even though she was well on the way to being drunk and would, without doubt, revisit her decision-making in the morning (or probably Monday morning, she was bound to have a heaving hangover tomorrow – not conducive to sound decision making), she felt that she had reached some critical milestones.

Suddenly Tim was by her side.

'I wonder,' he said, then appeared to start again, 'I mean..' He took a nervous sip of beer which went down the wrong way and sent him into a coughing fit. He drew a deep breath and smiled at her when he'd got it under control. 'I've never been any good at asking someone out on a date, so here goes; I wonder whether you'd like to have dinner with me sometime?' He said it quickly and a bit clumsily, but she loved it. She found his hand with hers and squeezed it. 'Yes,' she said. 'I think I would like that very much.'

Then the band were back. They went through some songs on the setlist to warm the crowd back up before Billy Watson announced that it was time for the request draw.

The first four draws were great selections but not what Mary wanted. Then, finally, Jamieson asked if he could draw the final request for the night. He did, and it was no surprise that 'Born to run' was pulled out. Claire watched as Jamieson caught Mary's eye and gave her a wink.

Claire later found out two things:

Mary had put in twelve requests for 'Born to Run' and,

Jamieson had pulled out a request for 'I just called to say I loved you', but *that* wasn't going to happen.

As soon as the band hit the song's first notes, Mary and Geoff stunned everybody by launching into what felt like a pre-rehearsed jive, but they swore it was improvised. The crowd opened up, and everyone cheered and clapped their hands. Tim shook his head in mock despair, but Claire could tell he was actually very proud that these two were his parents.

The band played on until, finally, Billy Watson quietened everything down. He spoke emotionally about losing his mother to dementia earlier this year. He thanked everyone for turning up this evening and hoped they had all had a great time. He explained that this year, for his Mum, he wanted to raise over ten thousand pounds for the Alzheimer's Society and that this year's final figure with ticket receipts, bar profits and donations was, wait for it, eleven thousand, two hundred and fifteen pounds plus some pence. Billy made a bowing, 'we're not worthy' motion to the crowd.

He thanked everyone again and wished them a Merry Christmas before, in his words, the night was about to reach its frenzied climax.

'Ladies and Gentlemen,' said Billy, arms spread wide ', I give you Mister Johnny Be Goode himself, the one, the only....

....Detective Inspector Alex Jamieson.'

The.

Crowd.

Went.

Wild.

Chapter Forty

Saturday, 11th December

The Wailing Bunnies setlist
   Saturday, December 11th - Charity night at the Bell pub
   Mr Brightside - Killers
   Heart of Glass (Liz vocals) - Blondie
   Jolene - (Liz vocals) - Dolly Parton (*in memory of Billy's Mum
Dolly - her favourite song*
   Night Fever - Bee Gees
   You should be dancing - Bee Gees.
   September - Earth Wind & Fire
   Laid - James (Tony vocals)
   ABBA medley - Dancing Queen/Knowing me, knowing
you/Mamma Mia (Liz vocals)
   Break and Raffle results
   Request spot (put list of options on tables before the
event) five, maybe six songs
   All I want for Christmas is you - M Carey (Liz vocals)
   Santa Claus is coming to town - Bruce.
   Merry Christmas, Everybody - Slade

Thanks for coming - figure for charity raised
Encore (grab someone special)
Summer Breeze
Encore, encore
Johnny B. Goode (DI Alex Jamieson)
Goodnight, and we love you all.

Epilogue

Monday 13th December – 07:00

Jason James sat back and closed his eyes.

He let the warmth of the sunshine flow over his face.

He loved living in Spain with its temperate winters – it certainly beat Bedfordshire and the cold, below-zero mornings that the locals faced there. Scraping ice from the car windscreen did not happen in southern Spain.

He was sitting on the terrace of his villa with a cup of coffee on the table in front of him. The time was seven o'clock. In his opinion the best time of the day. His wife and the kids were still in bed. He was waiting for Marty, a colleague from the football club, to arrive. They were due to go to a school and deliver a training session and, at the same time, see if there were any players that they could look at bringing into the club's academy. The programme was like the proverbial sausage machine – squeeze them in at the top and see what comes out at the bottom. The statistics suggested that for every twenty players the academy took on, one, possibly two, may find their way into the first-team squad. As you moved up the leagues, that figure reduced the higher you progressed.

Given his own personal experience, Jason knew how tough it was to carve out a career as a professional footballer. And just how painful it was to have your legs kicked from under you when you least expected it.

Sometimes life sucked.

His thoughts moved to Ash.

How just over a month ago, the world was the boy's oyster and how all it took was one swipe of a blade, whatever the circumstances behind it, to bring everything crashing down. A huge part of Jason died along with Ash that day. He had his own hopes and dreams for his son, and now, nothing. Well, not nothing. He had Spain and his family, but for now, his grief over Ash was pretty well all-consuming.

He thought of Lewis. He liked the kid and knew that he thought the absolute world of Ash. In his mind, he was acting out of misguided love for his half-brother. Jason wondered what would become of him, how the law would treat him. However you looked at it, the lad took a knife out with him and used it. Were there any mitigating circumstances? Jason hoped so.

He opened his eyes and found that, like most days since Ash's death, he had shed a few tears without realising it. He wiped his eyes on the back of his hand.

He was thankful, though. He knew he had got away with one, dodged a bullet, as they say.

He couldn't understand how the triumvirate of Holly, Mcniven and the Gatekeeper had spun him a line which he had taken hook, line and sinker. Surely his one brain carried far more significance than the three of theirs clumped together. But in this case, apparently not. He told himself that it was because he was too emotional at the time, not thinking straight, looking for vengeance for Ash.

And between them, they served up Michael Macklin.

Poor Michael Macklin, hardly innocent but certainly not responsible for what happened to Ash. Jason felt bad about how things had turned out but not enough to admit responsibility.

He recalled going to Holly's on the Friday and Holly's Oscar-nominated performance where she first let the name Michael Macklin slip—just planting a seed in his brain. Her Mother weighed in with her own opinions about the lad being a bad influence on Ashley, reinforcing her daughter's well-rehearsed words.

Then when Alex Jamieson unwittingly let slip that his team were considering factions at Akley FC as being involved, Jason's mind automatically leapt to Macklin.

By the time nerdy, nervous Davey Mcniven had phoned him on the Sunday afternoon, chuntering on about his concerns over Macklin and his potential involvement in what happened, Jason was sold. Macklin was responsible, and he had to pay.

Wow, the three of them had worked him over well and proper. In the knowledge that Lewis was responsible, they had presented him with Michael Macklin and wound him up, playing on his emotions, in the knowledge that he would respond.

And he did.

He stood outside the pub where Macklin was drinking for five hours in the pissing rain with a baseball bat shoved up the arm of his parka.

And when Macklin appeared – BAM – he took revenge for Ash – many times over.

Fortunately, he had the foresight to wipe his fingerprints from the bat and, in the knowledge that Mcniven rarely locked his car, stowed it away in the trunk, just in case the police should at some point search it.

That seemed to have worked. The last he had heard Mcniven was very firmly in the frame for what had happened to Macklin.

The doorbell rang.

Jason gathered up his empty cup and headed back through the patio doors. He called upstairs to his wife, 'see you later,' knowing that she would still be sleeping, and then detoured through the kitchen to load his dirty cup and saucer into the dishwasher.

On his way through the hall, he collected his kit bag, and as he opened the door, he started to say good morning to Marty, but he stopped short with a puzzled look on his face.

On his doorstep stood four men – two gardai from the local police force, a crumpled-looking middle-aged man and Detective Inspector Alex Jamieson.

Jamieson smiled and waggled the index finger of his right hand: 'Morning Jason,' he said, 'How's the finger you cut on Davey Mcniven's car boot?'

Printed in Great Britain
by Amazon

34064378R00148